UNDER HER SPELL

By the Author

Dreaming of Her

Under Her Spell

UNDER HER SPELL

by

Maggie Morton

2013

UNDER HER SPELL

© 2013 By Maggie Morton. All Rights Reserved.

ISBN 13: 978-1-60282-973-2

This Trade Paperback Original Is Published By
Bold Strokes Books, Inc.
P.O. Box 249
Valley Falls, NY 12185

First Edition: December 2013

CREDITS
Editor: Shelley Thrasher
Production Design: Susan Ramundo
Cover Design By Sheri (graphicartist2020@hotmail.com)

Acknowledgments

I would like to thank the amazing Radclyffe first, for running such a terrific company and for accepting my novel. I would also like to thank my very skilled editor, Shelley Thrasher, who has helped me to become a better writer. My thanks also go out to everyone at Bold Strokes Books, including Connie, Sandy, Cindy, and Toni. Thanks also to Sheri for yet another terrific cover. I would also like to thank Desiree for suggesting I write erotica all those years ago. Finally, I would like to thank Beanie for her help with editing and help being a better person, Bunky for his support and love, and Bucko for his support, love, affection, compassion, and acceptance—I love all three of you very, very much!

Dedication

To Beanie, who needs no magic to be magical

Chapter One

Terra glanced out her window again, seeing the moon was still full but a bit higher in the sky. Where was she? Athene was almost never late for their rendezvous, as punctuality was one of her many, many loveable traits. What could be keeping her?

But then Terra heard a soft knock on her door, and it slowly opened, and Athene entered the room on quiet, slippered feet.

"Are the bunny slippers new?" Terra asked.

"They were a regrettable gift from my aunt. She's visiting right now, so I've been wearing them around in the morning and at night. That's not the worst part, though."

"No? You mean something like hot-pink and lime-green striped bunny slippers with psychotic-looking googly eyes can get worse?"

"Yes," Athene said, easing herself down onto Terra's quilt-covered bed. "They used to squeak."

Terra laughed at that, then cleared her throat. "You poor thing. But…what do you mean 'used to'?"

"I kind of let Onyx chew on them last night—his idea, not mine. That cat is part devil, I sometimes think, but he's still helpful in my spells."

"I need more than a super-attentive familiar to help with mine," Terra said, not without a hint of disappointment in her tone.

Athene sighed, reaching out for Terra's hands and pulling her onto the bed to her right. "If only your mother..."

Then Terra let her face fall, her lips turning down into a sad pout. She had intended to use those lips for kissing tonight, and not much more. After all, it was their second-to-last night together before the goddamned quest, and they'd already said everything there was to say. About how they'd miss each other. About how worried they were about Terra's chances, since she had so little power, power that could have been practically immeasurable if it hadn't been for her mother...but no, Terra decided. Tonight was not for worries or sad thoughts about the past.

"I'd rather kiss you now than start crying," Terra said, her voice soft.

"Me too, my love." Athene cupped the back of Terra's head, her fingers flowing through Terra's short-cropped curls, their striking blue-black the first thing Athene had noticed about her—as she'd told Terra the first time they were alone and able to talk. That talk had led to late-night meetings in Terra's quarters, late-night meetings that led to amazing sex, and, after a while, amazing love.

Their first time together had not been the first time either of them had gone to bed with a woman, but it had been the first time Athene had come while in someone else's arms. She was amazed, she had told Terra, amazed at how well Terra's hands had worked her body...her *flesh*. And Terra, in turn, had been amazed at how aroused Athene had become, with only a few kisses against each breast, her hand buried between Athene's thighs—a hand that had gotten soaked in seconds, Athene's wetness dripping down those thighs as they kissed and touched and moaned, Terra whispering dirty things into Athene's ear as she worked her clit.

Maybe it was her words (Athene later told her no one had ever talked dirty to her before). Maybe it was the excitement and Terra's immense desire for her (she'd only had sex twice before, with two different—and, as she told Terra, seemingly disinterested—partners). And maybe they just had some sort of magical chemistry on that night, because Athene got Terra to come, too, her mouth tight on Terra's cunt, as Terra continued to talk dirty to her, growling word after word about how naughty she was, and how dirty she was, bedding down with one of the staff, one of the people who was normally far below her, and now *she* was the one servicing Terra, instead of the other way around.

After they'd both come an equal number of times, Athene turned to face Terra, a very serious look on her face. In an equally serious tone of voice, she'd told Terra that she didn't look at the staff the way Terra thought she did, and that while it had been hot while she'd been eating her out, "You shouldn't assume that I look down on you normally. You're far too beautiful for that, for one thing." Terra had turned her head down, a flush rising to her throat and cheeks, and Athene had told her she looked exceptionally cute when she blushed.

Terra was desperate to see her again after that, and the desperation was returned in kind, because that night turned into a long trail of nights, turning into over a year of amazing—but private—romance. And it came with many, many more nights just as hot as that first encounter.

But tonight would just be sex, because the love part was too painful. After all, Terra thought, as she began to unlace the front of Athene's silk nightgown, tonight would be their last night together for...well, best not to think about that. What an arousal killer, worrying about missing each other. No, instead, she chose to take in Athene's chest as her nightgown slipped off her breasts—breasts she couldn't find a single flaw in. Just like Athene's face, its shape narrow and delicate, with equally delicate features and the most kissable lips imaginable. Lips that she was kissing right now, kissing with a hunger she hadn't expected to have. She felt ravenous, starved for contact, her desire mounting so intensely it almost drew the breath out of her. And then, when Athene took her hand and placed it on her right breast, the breath *was* drawn out of her, a quick, loud, exhale of warm air, warm air that made Athene shiver as it hit her skin.

Or perhaps the shiver came from the feel of Terra's fingers on her nipple, gently twisting it back and forth, the nipple hard with arousal, arousal that Terra knew had spread down to her lower parts as well. She knew this from the way Athene began to squirm a little as she tweaked her nipple, which she did a little rougher than usual, but her roughness didn't get any complaints out of Athene. No, instead she got a gasp, and a soft, "Please…"

"'Please' what, my girl?" Terra was grinning now, loving the power she had, able to turn Athene on so easily. It had always been like that, unlike any of the women she'd been with before their first night together. And now, a year and a half in, nothing had changed. At least, nothing when it came to the sex they had. Their sexual experiences hadn't dimmed a bit. The orgasms, and everything else, had only gotten better.

"Please…please, I want you to be rough with me tonight."

"Sounds good to me." Only a little time passed before she grabbed both of Athene's wrists and slammed her to the bed. "So, you want to be my slut tonight? My whore? Is that what you want?"

"I've been reading some books, books with stuff like this in it, and they really, *really* turned me on." Athene looked down shyly when she said this, but with a fair bit of excitement on her face as well.

"You sly little coquette! You slutty little bibliophile!" Terra chuckled, a low laugh that seemed to hold an unusual touch of darkness in it. "Just say 'warlock' if I get too rough. The thought of a man should turn both of us off right away. Just say that and I'll stop." Then she sunk her teeth into Athene's shoulder. She didn't use an especially small amount of pressure. It was a test, to see exactly how much Athene could take and whether those books really did it for her as much as Terra hoped.

But Athene took it like a champ. She did shriek a little as Terra bit her, but it was a quiet shriek, and she said, "Thank you, mistress," as Terra loosened her mouth and then stopped. She didn't thank her when Terra bit her again, this time on the top of her left breast, this time a little harder. But Athene gave her the gift of a moan, because as Terra closed her teeth around her flesh, she also took her hands off Athene's wrists and started to grind her palm against her crotch. Terra's hand got incredibly wet as it worked away against Athene's panties, panties that were soaked through in an impressively short amount of time.

"You seem to like this, my lovely bottom."

"Yes, I must. I...I think I, um, more than just like it."

"That's good, because I really, really, really like it, too." As she growled each of those last six words, she ground her hand against Athene's panties, and when she finished her sentence, she slipped her hand inside them, finding that this was one fucking wet cunt.

"Goddamn, Athene, are you ever wet! You've *never* been this wet before. Seems like we've learned something new about you tonight." She slid her fingers down Athene's slit, finding a larger-than-usual clit in its certainly usual spot, and she began to rub it with her middle finger. With her other hand, she braided her fingers through Athene's long, full, golden hair, softer than silk and definitely far more beautiful. But she wasn't going to admire Athene's hair tonight, or compliment her in any way, unless it was to tell her how well-behaved she was, and how good she was at getting wet, and how pleasing it was to have such a submissive slut bottoming to her.

No, tonight Athene's hair was only a tool, one with which to control her. Terra did just that, grasping most of it in a tight fist and then yanking it back, hard, as she added another finger to Athene's clit.

Athene had already been moaning a little, but now she was getting louder and louder. Terra noticed that she looked nervous, too. "I'm worried that I'll get too...fuck! Too loud! Oh, God, I'm going to get so loud, so loud. Oh, I'm close, Terra, I'm close."

"Are you going to come for me, my little bitch? Am I going to steal an orgasm or two from that sopping-wet cunt of yours?" She couldn't help but be slightly surprised at the words that were coming out of her mouth, and how easily they were coming to her. They'd never done anything like this before. It had always been gentle until then—lovely, and very, very hot, but there had been no hair pulling, no biting, and only a small amount of name-calling.

But at the last second, Athene threw up her arms, and a bubble of light suddenly surrounded the bed. Terra realized then that Athene had almost never come that hard. Nor was she often this loud, her cries echoing off the glowing circle of light around them. And as Athene came, Terra's heart began to beat hard, because she almost couldn't stand how beautiful Athene looked in that moment of ecstasy.

Fuck, she thought. *Fuck, I'm going to miss her too much.* How was she supposed to get through the next however-many-days this stupid, goddamn, sucky quest would take? It was all for the best prize in the world, though, the best prize imaginable— Athene's hand in marriage.

It was Terra's turn next, and Athene's gentle touch—with just the right amount of pressure in just the right places, and especially at just the right times—drew all thoughts of the next day out of Terra's head, and she worried less and less each time she came.

But soon—far too soon, in her opinion—it was time for her lover to leave. Not just her lover, no, because very few people will risk their lives for someone they just enjoy falling into bed with. No, there was much more to their relationship than that. Far more, because as Athene kissed her good-bye, she took Terra's hand in hers, and when she released it, a glowing, ghostly band was wrapped around Terra's left ring finger.

"How sweet!" She smiled widely and thanked Athene as she quietly opened the bedroom's door and shut it slowly behind her. Sadly, it was time for them to both try to get some rest before the next day.

But after Athene left, and once she was back in bed, ready to sleep, Terra waved her hand over the ring, making it turn into mist and then disappear. It was too sad, however sweet Athene's gesture had been, to see a ring on that finger, a ring that might never appear for real. She still had just a little hope that she would be successful, that her disguise would work the next night and that not only would she be allowed to compete, but that she would win. One of her last thoughts before she drifted under was one of hope.

Magic, even the most powerful in the world, should never even try to match the magic of true love. But was she right?

CHAPTER TWO

Terra woke in the morning just as the sun had started lighting up her small bedroom. It was a little past six when she threw back the covers and put her feet onto the cold hardwood floor, shivering a little as it first touched her soles. It had been so much nicer under the covers, where she'd been daydreaming a bit about Athene. She had tried to push all thoughts of that night's banquet out of her head, but they'd come flooding in only a tiny bit after she first opened her eyes.

She went into her small bathroom and washed her face in the miniscule sink. The room didn't even have a bathtub, just a small shower with a glass door she kept spotless, a toilet, of course, and the tiny sink, with a small, mirrored cabinet above it that held her inexpensive toiletries. It was nothing like the bathrooms of the mansion's owners and, of course, their daughter, who just so happened to be Athene. Of all the women to fall for...but it was far too late to change her mind, now. She was more in love than she could quantify.

Terra shook her head at the thought that she could "change her mind" about such a thing. Silly, really, as her father had taught her when she was young that lovers weren't chosen so much as *they* chose *you*. Yes, Athene had "chosen" her with a single glance of her kind, beautiful eyes; just that one glance, and Terra was hers.

They'd barely crossed paths before Athene turned twenty; she'd practically been kept locked in her room, her parents were so over-protective. And Terra had spent her time in the stables with her father, Zachary, teaching her what he knew about math and science and the various arts as they fed and dressed the horses. He was one of the castle's gardeners as well, as the horses only had so many needs, and their riders' needs were limited as well. Zeus, Athene's father, almost never rode anymore because of his bad hip, and Cer, her mother, had never spent much time around animals of any sort since her birth. It was rumored that when Cer was born, every animal on the land died, and that she'd brought them all back to life with her touch. Of course, it was just a story, but the help did their best to keep her happy in every way possible. As happy as anyone could keep a woman as easily angered as Cer was, at least.

Terra didn't have to get started on her duties until seven thirty, so after putting on her usual work outfit, which consisted of a perfectly ironed white blouse and pale-gray slacks, she went down to the kitchen. Once there, she ate a quick bowl of oatmeal and picked up the sliced apple waiting by the door to the outside—the castle's cook always left one out for her in the morning—and she went down to the stables, her father's first stop on his ever-busy days.

"Hey, Dad." She leaned up against the stall where her father was brushing the mansion's prize stallion, a black Arabian named Djinn. Her father always brushed him until his coat shone, and he and Djinn would chat while he did. "Hey, D.J."

Djinn snorted. "Must you insist on calling me that, young lady?"

"You know I must, D.J."

"Hi, honey. How's your morning been so far?" Her father smiled at her, taking off his plaid newsboy cap and running his fingers through his shaggy, black hair. It had been said that she looked almost exactly like her mother, but Terra thought she had a fair amount of her father in her—her height, for one, as she was tall for a woman at five feet nine. And then there was their hair, although hers had hints of her mother's garnet-red locks in the form of subtle highlights throughout its blackness. And her father's nose, wide but still rather delicate, just like hers. To most, it would have seemed almost too feminine for a man, instead being almost perfect for a woman. Especially one on the slightly butch side of things, like her. But Terra's lips and eyes were both almost identical to her mom's—her eyes a blue that was almost silver, and her lips with slightly up-turned corners so that, unless she was frowning, she always seemed to have a slight smile on her face. Her father had told her that he appreciated seeing a bit of her mother in her face, but after the age of thirteen, the only way she had to compare herself to her mother's looks was in photos, because her mother wasn't with them anymore.

She hadn't been there since mere days before Terra's thirteenth birthday, the most important birthday for all of the Magic Ones. Because her mother had never been able to lead her through the magic-sharing ceremony that was supposed to always happen on each Magic One's thirteenth birthday, she'd received next to none of her mother's vast amount of magic powers. So her father was stuck in the stables and gardens, and she was stuck cleaning up after Athene's family, the Werths. Over the years, she'd come to accept that was just how it was, until she'd noticed Athene, of course.

Back in the present, Terra walked up to Djinn. "Want an apple?"

"Do you even need to ask, young lady?"

She took the apple out of her pocket and fed it to him, piece by piece, while she talked to her father. "So, do you have any special requirements for tonight's festivities?"

"Yes, keeping my one and only daughter out of harm's way." Her father frowned a little and started brushing the stallion a little harder.

"Aw, Dad…you know I'm set on doing this. You also know I love Athene, and she loves me, and this is the only way for us to be together."

"Are you certain they'll even accept a woman as her…" Zachary paused, then continued in a much lower voice. "As her wife? Even if you win? I mean, I know the world outside of ours is opening up to gay people like you and Athene, but your mother's people, the warlocks and witches, are all very old-fashioned. I'm not, of course," he was quick to add. "But I'm merely human. You know this. I'm very fond of Athene, though. Unlike the rest of her family, she's very kind to the help."

"Yes, Dad, and she's more than just kind to me."

"I know, sweetheart," her father said, looking up at her as he said this. He walked over to her and ruffled her hair a little. "I guess I should have realized I couldn't change your mind. Just as bull-headed as your mother."

"Yeah? I hope you mean that in a good way."

Zachary chuckled. "In the best way possible. I suppose I should ask if I can do anything to help?"

"Without magical abilities, you really can't." Terra hated to remind him of his humanity, but she herself was half human, so it wasn't such a blow coming from a half-breed like herself. "And with my own limited abilities, I'm really not sure…" She looked away into the distance.

"There is, though, the small, small chance that you might—"

She turned back toward him. "Might what?"

"I shouldn't, well, you'll find out soon enough. Hopefully." Her father leaned down just a bit and kissed her on the forehead. "It's really a shame, this being-human crap. I want so much for you to have it better, Terra. To have what you deserve, my shining example of a young woman. That's another way you're like your mom—not just your bull-headedness, but your good heart as well."

"And my bravery, too, I hope." Bravery that she was really going to need, starting that very night and continuing onto the terribly intimidating quest that would begin the very next morning.

She nuzzled Djinn and waved at Zachary. "I think I hear the dining hall calling me. It says I have at least five hours worth of cleaning, and some decorating to boot. I should be off, in other words."

"Sure, Terra. You be careful tonight, though. Promise?"

"Athene will keep an eye on me, keep me in line. Bye, Dad. I...I..."

"Me, too."

Her father put down his brush and walked Terra out of the stables. He took off toward the garden and she headed toward the door she'd exited through. The kitchen was the quickest way to the dining hall, of course. There would be plenty of tile-scrubbing in her near future, not to mention helping bring in countless deliveries and shine countless pieces of silver. She was not looking forward to her day's work, but she was still excited about the night that would follow all her work. She might have been slightly—or immensely—terrified about how it all might go, but she was still looking forward to seeing Athene all fancied up. After all, the woman looked *damn* good in a dress.

CHAPTER THREE

Terra's first chore was cleaning and waxing the large, single-paneled table in the dining hall. She had been shocked when she and her father had first moved to the mansion. She remembered thinking, *People actually live in places this big?* She'd been fourteen at the time, but that hadn't stopped the mansion's staff from putting her right to work. After all, as Isis, the female head of staff, had told her, teenagers usually had jobs in the human world, didn't they? A slight barb was hidden in the sentence, one Terra had caught, being used to the full-blooded witches and warlocks always seeing her as "lesser" than them.

Her treatment hadn't gotten much better with time, either. Even the lowest rung of the staff at the mansion was completely made up of supernatural beings, and only a select few of them treated her with any kindness at all. The chef, Freo, was one of the only ones there who treated her politely, which Terra thought might have been—at least partially—because she seemed to have a bit of a crush on Zachary. At least, it appeared that way, based on how many times Freo had complimented him, telling Terra what a skilled gardener he was, and how good he was with even the wildest of the horses. It was the only praise Zachary got, though, because Terra might have been lesser, but to them, the Magic Ones, her father was barely worth looking at.

He was entirely as skilled as Freo said, though, his obvious abilities in both the garden and the stables most likely the only reason he was kept around. Well, that and perhaps the fact that his wife, Terra's mother, had been one of the most powerful witches their kind had ever seen. It had been the only reason she had gotten away with marrying a mere human, because great magical power usually caused great intimidation, even if Nerit wasn't the type to use that to her advantage. She might have been dead for almost nine years, but she was still spoken of in reverent tones during the rare occasions she came up during the staff's conversations.

That didn't help Terra any, though, because she wasn't like her mother when it came to her magical abilities, not at all. She'd had to make do with a good work ethic in order to earn her room and board, her faint touches of magical ability only used to help a bit with ensuring the head-of-staff's orders were carried out to Isis's exacting standards.

She never allowed Isis to be disappointed in her, though, and that wasn't about to change today. After all, Terra might have had plans for that night, but until a bit before that night's soirée, she was on the clock, so she got out a sponge, filled a bucket with soapy water, and tucked a bottle of orange-scented wood cleaner under her left arm.

While she scrubbed the table clean, she lost herself in thoughts, thoughts and a long list of worries about that night, which was about all she could do to make the time spent cleaning seem to pass faster. Surprisingly soon, the table began to reflect the high ceiling's levitating chandeliers on its surface, a sure sign that Isis would, in her own prissy way, be pleased with Terra's work.

Next came the tiled floors. They were to be swept, washed, and waxed, and she did all three—in her own humble, human opinion—to perfection. As she'd cleaned the floors, she'd kept getting interrupted with flower deliveries coming in from the hall's open double doors, and she had placed each arrangement of orchids and baby's breath (a horrible combination, she thought) on the right end of the table until it almost seemed like the table would flip over from their weight.

Once she'd finished with the floors, it was off to the large kitchen, where a king's ransom of silverware would be waiting for her. Upon seeing it piled in a large, completely unsorted pile on one of the kitchen's tables, Terra couldn't even begin to stifle the large sigh that the grisly sight caused. Of course. She would have to sort it first, then shine it, and then—

"Hey, Cinderella, get the hell out of my way!" That extremely rude sentence had come from Thor, who should have had an "n" at the end of his name, because he was nothing if not a thorn in Terra's back. He'd taken a liking to her at first, but it was obviously a sexual liking, and once she'd shown him her complete and utter disinterest in bedding down with him, he'd started treating her like crap. Just as well, because she'd even prefer being treated like utter shit by him to being used as a place to bury his (most likely petite) "hammer."

Thor was carrying a very full pot of water to the stove, and he shoved her against a table with a rough elbow to her ribs. She groaned a little as she hit the table, and he smiled at her. "Watch where you're going and you won't need to be shoved out of the way, Cinderella."

It seemed he'd never read the entire story, Terra had thought when the nickname appeared, or he would have known that she became a princess at the end of it—a princess who could have happily dispersed with any staff members who had been cruel to her in the past. "*You* watch where *you're* going," she muttered, quietly enough that his large, ugly ears wouldn't overhear her retort. She glared at him, watching his flat-butted backside thankfully heading away from her. Between his presence and the gargantuan pile of silver, it was going to be an unpleasant afternoon. Oh well, at least she could have lunch first, along with some good company, because her only real friend on the staff, Freo, was walking back through the kitchen's windowed swinging door. As soon as she saw Terra, she grinned, her pretty, slightly chubby face lighting up.

"Honeybun!" Now that was a *much* better nickname, Terra thought, an equally wide grin spreading across her face that had, only moments ago, held a very angry grimace. She liked Freo just as much as she disliked Thor, which was to say a hell of a lot.

"Hey, Freo. What's cookin'?"

Freo laughed like she always did, even though Terra had greeted her that way since they had first met. Freo had taken an instant liking to fourteen-year-old Terra, telling her upon their first meeting that she was beautiful but far too skinny, and did she like chocolate-chip cookies? Terra had put on a bit of weight since then, perhaps more than she might have liked, but she'd never gotten a complaint about her body, just many, many compliments, especially from Athene. She grinned as she remembered the first thing Athene had said upon seeing her naked. "Fuck, your breasts are perfect!"

"You look like you might be having lascivious thoughts, Terra, by that flush that's rising up your neck." Freo was the only person besides Athene who could get away with saying such a thing. "Better either get a turtleneck or start thinking about food instead."

"Food? Did my favorite chef in the world just say 'food'?" She batted her eyelashes at Freo, who smacked her on the butt.

"Naughty girl. Come, follow me. I'll make you a chicken sandwich. Just tried a new bread recipe, and I think it turned out very well, and not a drop of magic used!" Freo prided herself on not using very much magic, a fact that made her rather disliked among the staff, but very much liked by Terra. And with food as good as hers always was, they begrudgingly gave her credit in the form of compliments mumbled around mouthfuls of food. Cer and Zeus approved of her food as well, as both of them had allegedly put on a few pounds when she joined the staff, she had told Terra.

The bread was amazing, and Terra finished the sandwich in no time at all, although that was partially because she was given only a fifteen-minute lunch break today. But she and Freo chatted away while she shined piece after piece of silver, the pile of unpolished ones slowly becoming dwarfed by the finished, perfectly sorted rows. Freo would bring her the occasional taste of food, a bite of beet drizzled with dressing, a bite of rich, dark chocolate, and she even sneaked her a small glass of wine right before Terra left. Of course, it wasn't from the mansion's cellars, but was instead from Freo's own collection, as she had started growing some grapes by her cottage shortly after she'd started there.

Terra wondered, sometimes, what the wine from the cellar tasted like, but the only kind she'd ever had was Freo's, and all that really mattered was that it tasted damn good to Terra. She and Athene had gotten tipsy on it a few times, leading to fumbling but still hot encounters in Terra's room. They'd been more adventurous than usual those times, including one particular night where Terra had talked Athene into letting her finger her ass. That hadn't been the last time she talked her into it, though, and that was the thought Terra kept in her head as she helped a few male servants set the table in the dining hall.

Many more tasks followed, and Terra was almost too exhausted to think by the time it was seven thirty. But she had to sharpen her brain, because a lot would be asked of the poor, exhausted thing in the hours to come. Just as she finished her last sip of some wine she'd snuck from under Freo's nose, her door swung open and there was Athene, carrying a silver garment bag and wearing a gorgeous, silk, and (thank the Goddess) low-cut gown. It went down to her knees, showing off part of the legs that had been pressed up against Terra only a number of hours ago, and she now had to convince herself that a quickie was a very, very bad idea.

"I think we should have a quickie," Athene said, and Terra cracked up.

"A woman after my own heart!"

"Or the area a ways beneath it. Anyway, while the spell kicks in, I think I should go down on you. It'll take about ten minutes, and I want your entry into being a man to be pleasant."

"Because being one won't be?"

"Not to the best of my recollection."

"You mean you—"

"I'm kidding, sweetie. Now, get undressed. And fast, because I need to be back there in ten minutes, or my parents might notice that my body double isn't too interactive. I put her in a living-room chair reading some poetry, so that should hold them off for a while. They may not be perfect, but they do know how I love a good book."

"That you do. And you know I love you more because of it. Well, if I *must* have sex with you, we should probably get it over with."

Athene grinned, dropping the garment bag on the bed. Then, her hips slowly swishing from side to side (in a rather lovely way, Terra thought), she sashayed her way over to Terra, until she stood only about half a foot away.

Terra barely had time to unbutton her blouse before Athene's hands rushed toward her, and almost too quickly, she undid the button on Terra's slacks. Next she unzipped them, and finally, in one quick, deft movement, she yanked them down, Terra's black cotton panties too, all the way down to her ankles.

Shoving Terra's legs apart, she forced Terra to stumble just a little, because it was almost like her ankles were bound together, her bunched-up slacks hobbling her and making moving with any sort of grace (or speed) completely impossible. She had grown wet very quickly, the excitement of Athene's control over her convincing her they would definitely have to play this game again, sometime in the near future.

And then, her wrists were grabbed and held tight against her sides, Athene's expert tongue getting right to work on her quickly hardening clit. Athene had her moaning almost immediately, as her tongue almost never made a mistake. And yes, it wasn't making any *this* time. She was growing a bit wetter, becoming a bit more turned on with each flick and lick of the long, agile tongue that had gotten her off countless times before. It wasn't going to fail either of them this time. That much was obvious to Terra, as she had noticed her body was already tightening, even though only a mere minute had passed since Athene had begun to eat her out.

She stiffened some as Athene placed two fingers at her opening, tensing in anticipation for the moment that was coming, when those two fingers would first slip inside her hole. Then that moment came, and every inch of her tension left in almost an instant, quickly replaced with an intense and almost desperate need to come.

But this might be the last time they could be together in this way until the quest was over, and so it needed to last, at least for a while longer. "Slow...down," she gasped, dangerously close to the edge.

"You want me to *tease* you, then?"

Goddamn, Terra thought, what had gotten into Athene? Whatever it was, she thought, as she turned her quivering lips up into a wicked, happy smile, where had it been all her life? Athene's tongue slowed to a crawl, and Terra almost instantly regretted her words…mostly, at least. Athene's tongue started at the top of her slit and then inched its way down, down, until it met the place where her fingers had entered Terra's body. Those fingers began to slide out ever so slowly, until just the very tips of them remained inside her.

A sudden, hard thrust from them made Terra cry out. She was desperate to find something to squeeze, desperate to find some way to hold on, if only for another few seconds. No, it was too soon, far too soon! But there it was, a rich, full orgasm, bleeding out from her cunt and almost making her topple over.

Athene held her up, though, her hand gripping Terra's sides, and then Terra felt something strange. It almost seemed as if her body was changing, and with a glance down, she saw that yes, it was! They'd planned to disguise her as a man at the dinner, but, motherfucking hell, did that really have to mean she'd have a man's *chest* the whole evening?

"You don't look happy, sweetie," Athene said, rising from her knees and walking over to where she'd dropped the silver bag.

"What, you thought I wanted a man's torso to go along with the stubble and Adam's apple? A *hairy* man's torso?" Her voice came out a fair number of octaves lower than usual—a male voice, of course, to go along with her brand-new male body. She looked down at her boob-less, icky chest, giving it a very well-deserved scowl.

"The spell kind of comes with one, I'm afraid. I didn't want to tell you, because…I thought you would react pretty much like you are right now. If it helps," Athene said, unzipping the garment bag and taking out an expensive-looking three-piece suit and emerald-green dress shirt, "I decided to make you nice and muscled."

"Yeah, like having a *more* manly chest is going to make me happier. Well, in for a dime, in for a dick, I guess." Then she quickly grabbed at her crotch. Thank the Goddess, she still had an entire, fully working cunt. If Athene had decided to give her a dick along with everything else, she would have…she would have…Well, she would not have been happy, at the very least.

Athene laughed. "Since your work shoes are already super-butch, I thought I'd just give them a magic polish and have you wear them tonight. I made sure your feet are the same size as usual."

"How will anyone know how well-endowed I am if I have tiny lady-feet?"

Terra was grinning now, but she stopped the moment she saw Athene start turning toward the door. She couldn't help it. She had to have one last kiss. She shuffled her way over to where Athene stood and said, "Change me back, just so I can kiss you." Athene touched her arm, and Terra felt her body changing again, back to its normal form. She gave Athene a hard, passionate kiss, one that also had a fair bit of tongue thrown in. "So that's what I taste like today," she murmured as she slowly pulled her lips away.

"Anyone ever tell you how good of a kisser you are?"

"I learned from the best."

Athene let go of her arm then, and her body grew and changed back to that of a man. When the room held only her once again, a lump rose in her throat and she tried to swallow it, hoping no tears would come. She had to keep herself together tonight, because this was a huge risk, these actions she was taking. A huge risk, yes, but a very, very important one. She stiffened her shoulders and straightened her back, cracking her much larger, much hairier hands. Then she walked over to her closet and got out her lady-shoes. This shit was *on*.

CHAPTER FOUR

First she had slipped out a mostly ignored door near her first-floor bedroom, and then she'd come around to the front doors of the mansion. Straightening her silk tie—which was something she'd never done before, so was she doing it right?—she rang the doorbell and tried to put an entitled expression on her face. She was pretty much certain that the other six men who would be attending this shindig and competing against her would be rich, spoiled brats. After all, each of them came from one of the most powerful families in the Magic Ones' world, because Zeus and, of *course*, Cer, obviously wouldn't settle for anything less. Not for their gifted, beautiful daughter, no sir, no way.

But none of the other men were already in love with her, and none of them had received her love in return. If only that had been enough, Terra thought. But no, they had to have this ridiculous quest put in place, blocking her from Athene…and Athene from her.

The door opened, and there stood the butler, Eshu. She had always thought him to be handsome, and he was less rude to her than most of the staff, so she almost liked him. But now, shockingly, he bowed his head slightly, a move that stated that, for once, he thought she had the upper hand. "Saturn, I presume?"

"Y-yes, that's right." Of course. It wasn't *her* that had the upper hand, but Saturn, a man who, before this night, hadn't even existed, until Athene had planted him and his life story into the head of everyone who would be in the mansion and at this night's incredibly important event.

He opened the door wider and gestured toward the entryway. "Enter, if you please. May I take your jacket, sir?"

"Sir"? Terra could easily get used to being treated with respect around here, but she never, ever wanted to get used to being called "sir."

"Thank you, Es...esteemed butler of the Werths."

Eshu cocked an eyebrow at her strange words, but he clearly decided to ignore what she had said, because he bowed even more deeply as she walked past him. She handed him her coat, and as she entered the house's main living room and saw six sets of male eyes focus on her, she started to wish she'd come in a coat of armor instead. She might not have had any magic to back it up, but at least she would have looked tough to those six creepily assessing sets of eyes. And those sets of eyes belonged to six very attractive young men, all of whom, she realized now, happened to be her competition.

Zeus and Cer were seated on a royal-purple loveseat, each of them holding a stemmed glass of what must have been champagne. Both Zeus and Cer had always dressed impeccably, and the same was true tonight, Zeus in a sleek pinstriped suit and Cer in a lavender-colored, satin sack dress, with matching shoes that had red soles. *Those* must have cost a pretty penny, Terra thought, and then that thought went *poof* as her body tightened, and not in a good way. There was her least favorite person in the world—Isis, the head of staff—whose not-very-well-hidden dislike for her had only grown with time.

She walked up to Terra as soon as they made eye contact, her stilettos clicking against the tile floor in a rather ominous way.

But instead of berating Terra like she usually did, Isis handed her a glass of champagne and said, "Welcome to the Werths' home. You must be Saturn. It's a delight to meet you, sir."

Even if it was the wrong word, Terra thought, she was really starting to like this "sir" business. Now, if only she could run into Thor tonight, too, she wouldn't mind *him* calling her "sir." Maybe if she did see him, she'd pinch his ass for good measure, as he'd done the same to her a few very unpleasant times.

Cer turned her dark eyes toward Terra as she walked farther into the room. She smiled. It was a cold smile, but the first one Terra had ever received from her. She watched Athene's mother as she gracefully rose from the loveseat and walked over to her. "Saturn, it's a delight to finally meet you. I've heard so many good things about your family, the…the…oh my, I can't believe I'm forgetting your last name! How embarrassing!" Cer looked like she was attempting to look embarrassed, too, but she didn't quite pull it off.

Then Cer put out her hand, but instead of shaking it, Terra brought it to her mouth and gently placed her lips against it. "What a delight it is to meet you, Madame Werth."

"Please, call me Cer. After all, we might be family soon!" Cer tittered. Terra attempted to laugh too, and a manly chuckle, albeit a fake-sounding one, roared out of her mouth. It was a little too loud, she realized, as a few people turned toward her as soon as it left her lips.

She coughed into her fist, then cleared her throat. "Ahem. A delight to meet you, *Cer*, then. And would that beautiful woman in the corner be your daughter?"

"Yes, that's my darling Athene, talking to Pan Humphries, in the white, embroidered shirt, and Eros Flint, the man with the gorgeou…with the wavy brown hair. He may wind up being your main competition, from what I know of his family and their abilities."

"Well, I'll be sure to introduce myself to him, then. And Athene, as well. After all, I want to see if her personality matches her looks."

"Oh my, Saturn," Cer said with a forced-looking grin, showing off her far-too-perfect teeth, "you are *too* bold!"

Terra walked over to where the two men stood talking to Athene. Mine, Terra thought as she made eye contact with her girlfriend. *Or, at least, she should be.*

Eros and Pan turned toward her as she walked up to them. "Hello, Athene. My name is Saturn. You look beautiful in that dress." She took Athene's hand in hers and kissed its back—an action she thoroughly enjoyed with *this* particular person's hand.

"Thank you. You must be Saturn. I like your manners, so old-school." Athene gave her a gentle smile, very different from the one that had been on her face before they'd made eye contact.

"Glad you approve. And you must be Pan...and Eros?"

Each man nodded at her as she said his name, and she felt an instant liking toward Pan. He had a warm smile, with a touch of crow's-feet around his eyes, and he was wearing the best shirt in the whole room, with what looked to be the Blue Willow pattern embroidered across its front in dark-blue thread. "I like your shirt," Terra told him. "My mother used to have a whole set of Blue Willow china she used for special occasions."

"Thanks. Mine prefers chintz, which I find a little flashy for my taste."

No wonder she had liked him. She could tell now, almost for sure, that he was "part of the family." Great, so now the lesbian was competing against a gay man for a supposedly straight woman's hand in marriage. "Just ridiculous," Terra muttered under her breath.

"What was that?" Eros asked. His eyes were full of intelligence, which in the magic community usually meant the person was full of power, too.

"Nothing. Just wondering when dinner will start."

"Oh, are you not enjoying this lovely young woman's company?" he asked, his tone mirthful.

"Of course I am, Eros. It was just a long drive from my home, and I have heard the Werths' chef is exceptional at her craft."

"If you say so." Eros's playful smirk turned to a slight sneer as he turned back toward Athene, but she was looking at her parents, and Pan was looking at his feet, so only Terra saw a glimmer of lust in his hazel eyes. He might have been good-looking, but that was no excuse for him to think he was handsome enough to get away with looking her girlfriend up and down like she was a delicious piece of meat.

Terra pretended to stumble and slammed her petite foot down onto Eros's.

"Ouch!"

"Oh, excuse me! My lack of food and this delightful champagne seem to have gone straight to my head." She downed the last of her bubbly and bowed slightly at Athene. "It was very nice to meet you, Athene. Now, I believe I'll ask the lady of the house where the bathroom is, so I can freshen up before dinner." Terra turned and walked away, smiling a little as she headed back toward Cer.

Chapter Five

The dinner that night was the first time Terra had eaten the same meal as the Werths. The *exact* same meal. She couldn't help the small bit of jealousy that rose when she compared her normal dinner to this...this exceptional feast.

First came a beet salad, with hazelnuts, a delicate—but still pleasantly assertive—dressing, and shaved black truffle on top. Then there were fig-prosciutto turnovers, topped with a thyme-laced béchamel sauce. After that came foie gras with dried cherries and Brie, which was a little rich for her taste. As were the Werths, admittedly, she realized. If this plan worked, if they accepted her into their family, would she really want to live the way they did? Their every wish and desire fulfilled by their staff? Endless amounts of money? Daily meals of this quality and abundance?

Admittedly, the food part sounded okay to her. But the rest? No, it was all—ha ha ha—too rich for her commoner blood. Some people would weep at their distance from this level of opulence, were they to work for the Werths, but although she wouldn't have complained about receiving a fair bit more respect from the people surrounding her, she didn't want deference and "Yes, ma'am," and "Whatever you say, ma'am," and "Of course I'll walk over hot coals barefoot for you, ma'am." No, she really liked being a commoner, and when she glanced at Athene, who was laughing at something Pan had just said, she hoped Athene wouldn't mind stepping away from all this luxury and living a simpler life. She'd never asked Athene about their future, as, until they'd hatched this plan together a number of weeks ago, they'd never imagined they had one. But perhaps they would be able to discuss it someday. Someday soon, because the quest started the very next morning, Terra reminded herself, a thought that came with a slight tightening throughout her entire body.

"So," Eros said, as he cut into his Kobe steak, "what does your family do, Saturn? I've heard of them, of course, but I can't seem to recall what the...the...your family's business is."

Fuck. Not only had they forgotten to work a last name into the spell, but they'd also forgotten to work in the way "Saturn" and his family had come by their wealth. She quickly shoved a large bite of meat into her mouth to stall while she invented whatever it was they did. After all, the Magic Ones thought they should come by their money honestly. It was a surprising shared belief among their kind, probably started by their first two members, Anshar and Kishar. They were two Mesopotamian villagers who rose to be thought of as godly because of their magic and, apparently, their rise from destitution to great—and almost immeasurable—wealth.

But all good things must come to an end, as did Terra's large bite of beef, and so she had to give him the answer he had requested. She told him the only lie she'd been able to come up with. "They're in the sheep business."

"*Sheep? Really?*" Eros laughed. "That sounds like a very baaaaaahd joke, to me," he said, still laughing away.

"Yes, sheep. Sheep, which just happen to have the finest wool and meat in the country. In any country, actually. They ship our meat and wool worldwide, from here in the States all the way to Europe and Asia. Our wool is so superior we could practically sell sweaters in the Sahara Desert midsummer." She wiped the sides of her mouth and took a small swallow of her wine. "Haven't you heard of Carrigan Sheep?"

Eros looked confused for a moment, but then Athene reached past him for the salt, brushing against his arm as she did. He looked down at his arm, then back up at Terra, and said, "Oh, yes, I suppose I have." He still looked mildly confused, but at least he believed what she'd said.

Close call, Terra thought, almost wanting to sigh in relief.

Dessert consisted of a delicious chocolate torte, decorated with shaved dark chocolate and gold leaf. Terra had seen the tortes being made, of course, as she and Freo talked and she shined piece after piece of stupid silverware. She couldn't believe that every utensil at the table she now sat at had been cleaned and put in place by her and one of the maids. Nor could she believe that she was passing for one of "them" and being allowed to use the Werths' finest silver to eat their finest food.

Once everyone's dessert plates were empty, Zeus rose from his chair and tapped his wineglass with his dessert fork. "Men—shall we adjourn to the living room for some of my finest cognac? And perhaps some...Cuban cigars? Don't tell anyone," he added with a wink.

Terra hated cognac almost as much as she hated cigars, but she choked down a small glass of the first and puffed away at the second. She had to blend in, after all. Also a little unpleasant for her was being in a room full of men—or at least these particular men. Eros was the least pleasant, of course, and Pan the most, so she stayed away from Eros and stuck near Pan, chatting with him about his love of sailing and how he wanted to take off for a year and go around the world.

"With...with Athene, perhaps?"

"Yeah, something like that," Pan replied, a slightly wistful look flickering across his face.

Just then, Zeus rose from his chair and placed his empty snifter on the table beside it. "I think we should all retire to our rooms now, as it is getting late and I want you all well-rested when it comes time to take off tomorrow. Your cars will be brought around to our driveway at seven a.m., and I will make sure you all have one of our chef's wonderful croissants and a cup of nice, strong coffee as well. You'll be needing all the help you can get, I'm sure!"

Then Zeus raised his arms into a V-shape, looking much scarier than he usually did. His voice boomed out with his next words, and she watched, mouth agape, as a small, dark storm cloud appeared over his head, flashes of lighting and booms of thunder emanating from it. In a deep, intimidating voice, he called out, "Your quest will be thus: you will vanquish a foe with wings, find a river of great power and drink from it, make it rain in the desert, and lastly, locate Zeus's hidden goblet."

Zeus's hidden goblet? It almost seemed as if he was someone else in that moment. And perhaps he was.

The storm cloud gave one last, loud boom of thunder and disappeared. Zeus's arms dropped then, and his normal smile returned to his face. "That must have been the quest's requirements for you lot, because I was somewhere else for a few moments. Ha! One last thing, and then it's time for you to sleep…if you can," he added with a slightly sinister chuckle. "While some of you may already know this, your quests may differ. Slightly, vastly, who knows?" He shrugged in what seemed to be a playful way, and then he turned and began to walk toward the stairs that led to his bedroom.

Terra glanced around at the six men still in the room. She'd learned most of their names by now, and it sounded like she might be seeing some of them again. Eros seemed like the one to watch out for, but so did a slender, dark-haired man named Zao Jun Sòng. He didn't make her skin tingle the way Eros did, but Zao Jun was still the only other man in the room who put off a noticeable amount of power. Besides Zeus, of course, but he kept his power contained better than the two young men, and Terra only felt it whenever he was angry at one of the staff and began to tear them down for a perceived fault in their performance. A perceived fault that was usually real, so at least he got angry for, mostly, the right reasons. Terra might have been a little afraid of him, but he treated Athene well, from what she'd told her. Much better than Cer did, as Athene had also told her of Cer's noticeable standoffishness when it came to her. The fact that she loved Athene barely showed, she had said, and when it did, the signs of her love were gone just as quickly as they had appeared.

But now it was off to her bedroom, hopefully to see Athene one last time before she took off the next day. Athene had promised to take care of the car part of things, and she said that Terra was in for a treat, as she was going to transform Terra's cantankerous, lime-green VW Bug into a mint-condition 1966 Jaguar E-Type coupe, which, although Terra wasn't exactly a car aficionado, was still a damn gorgeous piece of work. This was also apparently one of the rare occasions that Athene would be needing the help of her familiar, a Siamese cat named Onyx. He'd started out in life black, but Athene had decided she didn't want to be a walking stereotype, so with her father's help, she changed him into a sleek, attractive Siamese, something Onyx had never forgiven her for.

This night, and only this night, Terra would be sleeping in a much, much nicer room than usual. One of the Werths' staff led her to her temporary quarters and turned down the four-poster bed for her. The sheets were silk, not cotton, and everything in the room obviously cost a pretty penny. But everything was much more ornate than she liked, almost to the point of tackiness, and as she climbed into the bed after stripping off all of her clothes, she found herself missing the simplicity and comfort of her own room. Not to mention having her own body, as she glanced at her grossly hairy pecs with a mild shudder of disgust.

Then a door near the bed swung open, and Terra jumped. But seconds later she saw a familiar, strikingly beautiful face, and she found she had no reason at all to be scared. Not when it was Athene walking toward her, looking like she was very, very happy to see Terra alone. And then, with a wave of Athene's hand, her body became her own again, and she groped her chest to make sure her boobs were still the same size.

"Nice to have those awe-inspiring tits back," Athene said, stripping off her satin pajamas and climbing into the bed beside Terra. She was wearing only her panties now, lace and see-through, showing off the slight amount of bush she always left in place. The *lovely* amount of bush she always left in place, Terra was thinking, her eyes happily taking in Athene's delicious, tempting crotch as they lay there side by side.

"Something about having you at arm's length all night has made me hungry for your pussy," she told Athene. "May I?"

"Something about you having a man's body all night long has made me hungry for your tits. And yes, you may. In fact, I'll help you out." Athene took Terra's hand and turned around until her ass and back were pressed up against the front of Terra's naked body, her flesh feeling all at once firm and plush, soft and hard, the perfect combination for Terra's arousal.

Athene took control then, sliding both of their hands into her panties. "Help me get off, just this one last time, this last time before you leave tomorrow morning. Give me some good memories of your touch." She moved her hand beneath Terra's, and Terra felt Athene's fingers begin to move against her clit, flicking back and forth, circling beneath Terra's hand.

Terra decided to take control. She gripped Athene's hand, slowing her down, only letting her move at what was hopefully a painfully slow pace. Athene made a low, soft sound of pleasure as Terra guided her hand against her cunt, Athene's hand completely under Terra's control. "Do you really like when I take over like this?" Terra wanted to make sure that, not only was Athene enjoying herself, but that she was enjoying herself as immensely as Terra was. The act of taking control of Athene's hand and Athene's pleasure caused Terra's body to tense behind her, her limbs growing tight with need and the distinct hunger for pleasure…for *more* pleasure.

"An unbelievable amount, apparently." Athene answered a few moments later, as she shoved her body against Terra's naked front, a very obvious sign that her words were likely one-hundred percent true—one-hundred percent, at the very least.

"If that's true," Terra replied, "then I want you to slip those dripping wet fingers I'm holding in between those beautiful lips of yours. I want you to taste yourself." Still gripping Athene's hand, Terra moved it up over her body, rubbing Athene's wet fingers against her stomach and then the crevice between her breasts, all the way up her neck and past her chin and against her lips. "Open them."

Terra felt those lips part, and then she pushed their fingers into Athene's mouth, spreading it wide and filling it. Terra felt Athene's tongue slicking up all of those fingers, twisting against them as she moaned around the six fingers that were busy spreading apart her lips and filling her mouth. "That taste good, sweetheart?" Terra asked, and Athene shuddered against her as she spoke. "Do you taste good?" she asked again.

"Mmm" was Athene's answer, the sound vibrating against Terra's fingers, the sound making her own cunt heat up, and her breath caught in her throat for just a moment from the sudden, intense arousal that Athene's moaning caused.

"Let's get you off now, then." Terra dragged their fingers back down Athene's body, all the way back down to her clit, and she let her have almost free rein this time, just enjoying the feel of Athene writhing against her every few moments, clearly getting off on all they'd done. Then Athene—tense, taut, and ready—began to shudder and quake against her as Athene came with a low, lengthy growl.

"My turn now?" Terra purred into Athene's ear.

"How can I say no? There's just…no way, not after I've come as hard as that. You know how pliable a good orgasm makes me, sweetie." Athene flipped around and brought her lips to Terra's, kissing her much harder and much more passionately than usual, kissing her like…well, like they weren't going to see each other for a while. If the sex was this good right *before* she left, Terra thought, it'd probably be fucking amazing when she got back. Then came an unexpected, terrifying thought. Would she make it back? But when Athene brought her gentle fingers to one of her nipples, and her lips to the other, that thought dissolved in almost an instant.

"That's good, honey, that's so, so good…" Terra tilted her head back as those lips began to suck harder, and as those fingers began to twist and tweak her other nipple, she shoved her leg between Athene's, thrusting against her cunt as Athene sucked away. Then Athene removed her mouth and, slowly, let her lips drift down Terra's body, kissing her here and there in a gentle, almost hesitant way.

It was different from how they'd begun, but Terra wasn't even close to complaining, especially not when those lips stopped at the best spot imaginable. Athene kissed her where her lower lips first began to part and then slipped her tongue out of her mouth and gave Terra's cunt a long, slow, sloppy lick. She started to eat Terra out then, her mouth's ministrations more than welcome, more than skilled, more than enough, because after a while, she brought Terra over the edge, not stopping until Terra had come not once...not twice...but three times in quick, perfect succession.

After that third time, she pulled Athene up the mattress until they were face-to-face. "I'm really, really going to miss you, you know. We've never spent this long apart."

"I *do* know," Athene told her. "And I'm really, really going to miss you, too. But I'm afraid I have to get back to my own room. I'll see you in the morning, and I'll make sure Freo packs you something better than what everyone else is getting in their breakfast to-go bags."

"Knowing Freo, that won't take too much arm-twisting."

"Of course not," Athene said, getting out of the bed and pulling her nightgown over her head. "She loves you—it's obvious. Just like it's obvious that I love you." She raised her hand to her mouth as it stretched into a yawn. "I'm off to my own bed then. Sleep well, and good luck, if I don't get to say that to you tomorrow."

"I'm gonna need it," she mumbled after Athene had left. "I'm going to need all the luck I can get. All the luck..." But before she could finish that sentence, she drifted into a deep and delicious sleep. When the rising sun woke her up, she found herself wondering if she would be able to sleep at all while she was apart from Athene.

CHAPTER SIX

The car was a true beauty, Terra thought. She also thought it was much more attractive than she was, back once again in her man-disguise. On her walk to the car, she was carrying an embroidered lunch bag and large travel mug, full of coffee that she knew would be important fuel for the beginning of her trip—of her *quest*. She wasn't tired in the least, not after that lovely night of sleep she'd gotten, but still, the thought of what might be asked of her, considering her distinct lack of magical ability...it was a rather exhausting thought.

The men had drawn straws to see who would exit the driveway first, and surprisingly, Terra had drawn the longest one. She got into her lipstick-red Jag and started the ignition with the keys she usually used for the car's previous incarnation, her ugly, inferior Beetle. Poor Beetle, she thought as she shifted the car out of park and into drive. You can't compete with a *real* classic, can you?

Her brand-new monogrammed travel bag was already on the front passenger-side seat, and she glanced at it, wondering why people would pay so much for just a piece of luggage. The car, though, she could understand.

So. Here she was, and it was time to leave the driveway, to take off and go wherever her heart led her. Right now, she was trying to convince it that yes, even though she was leaving her love behind, she'd be back soon enough, and then they could truly be together.

The quests were an age-old ritual for the daughters of the witches and warlocks, another thing they had to thank their ancestors for. If only Terra could have traveled back in time and given them a lecture on the importance of true love and the importance of letting women make their own decisions. But that was impossible, at least for Terra, and most likely for even the most powerful of the Magic Ones.

It's now or never, she thought as the engine idled, its sound almost like that of a purring cat. *Now or never…*

After one glance at where Athene stood on the mansion's front lawn, she turned back toward the road and moved her foot onto the gas. You can't change the past, she thought, but you still have some control over the future. Even without the help of magic.

Once she reached the end of the driveway, she turned right onto Whippoorwill Avenue, because did it really matter which direction she took? She would probably know soon enough if it was the right one.

She watched in her rearview mirror as each man's car pulled out of the driveway, some going toward her car and some in the opposite direction. Zao Jun was right behind her in a black Mercedes, and he was quickly catching up. She started driving a little faster, and then, after turning right onto Howard, she lost him. Thank the Goddess.

A few miles down the street, low, thick fog began to flow onto the road ahead of her. It got thicker and thicker with each cross street she drove past, until she couldn't see a single damn thing in front of her. Or behind her, or to her left or right. And this didn't seem to be normal fog, either, because when had fog ever filled up the streets of her city? It never had while *she'd* lived there. Not even once.

She slowed to a crawl and did her best to concentrate. Her stomach gave a low growl, but it would have to be patient, because what if her trip ended prematurely due to a car accident? That just wouldn't do.

Once she had slowed to fifteen miles an hour, she realized something—she couldn't hear anything other than her car. There should have been sounds of traffic behind her, because a fair number of vehicles had been on this street when she'd turned onto it.

Her stomach growled again. "Shut up, stomach. You'll have to be patient."

"I certainly hope not, Terra," came a voice from the backseat. "Athene forgot to feed me before she sent me out to your car."

"Holy fuck!" She slammed on the brakes. No, that hadn't been *her* stomach. It had been someone else's, someone else whose voice sounded very familiar, which was a funny choice of word since, as she watched, Onyx slowly appeared in the middle of the backseat.

"You bastard! You scared me half to death!"

"We were going to tell you, of course, but they kept Athene so busy these last few weeks she just completely forgot about it, until I reminded her this morning." He raised a paw and gave it a couple of licks. "There. Much better. Anyway, I'm here now, my dear, and you can't do much about it. Especially since we aren't in Kansas anymore, my fellow friend of Dorothy."

"What do you mean?" Terra narrowed her eyes as him. She liked Onyx, she really did, but she was having a hard time remembering that right now. After the way he'd scared the living shit out of her, she didn't think anyone would really blame her.

"Look around, sweetheart. Just look around."

And he was right. They were in the middle of a two-way, paved road, with grassy hills off to each side of it. She looked at her watch. A whole hour and a half had passed since she'd left the Werths' driveway, and she saw no sign of the city she'd just left. Though maybe, she thought with a small smile, this just meant she was getting a head start on the quest.

"Why don't I pull us off this road—or whatever it is—and see if Freo packed anything you might enjoy. Although I doubt there's any cat food in this lunch sack."

Each of their stomachs growled again, almost in unison, and so without waiting for an answer from Onyx, she pulled the car off the road and killed the motor.

Before Terra opened the lunch bag, a strange tingling crossed her skin, and her arms shrank back to their normal size, her hands her own again, too. A glance in the rearview mirror showed her that yes, she was a woman again.

More than ready for breakfast, she unzipped the lunch bag. Then she let out a laugh. Inside of it was a scone, a baggie of bacon, and yes, not one, but two cans of cat food. "That silly Athene, forgetting to tell me but remembering to tell Freo. I guess it's more important that you're fed than it is for me to actually be in on the joke."

"I agree, although I hardly think you could call me joining your quest a joke. More like a divine gift."

"Whatever. Let's just agree to disagree and eat breakfast."

"Gladly."

Terra opened his cat food and moved her bag to the backseat, placing the can in its previous spot on the seat next to her. Onyx climbed over the armrest and settled down next to the can of food, starting in on it before Terra had even taken her scone out of the bag.

Once she had, though, and once she'd taken her first bite of it, she moaned appreciatively. "Best. Scone. Ever," she mumbled around the bite of delicious baked goods. It was her favorite kind, blueberry-walnut, with hard, crunchy sugar crystals on top. The coffee was great too, hazelnut with tons of cream, just how she liked it. And the bacon was much higher quality than the kind she was used to getting from the kitchen, fatty and oh-so-rich-tasting.

The two of them ate in companionable silence for a while, just enjoying their food, and then Onyx looked up from his empty cat-food can. "I don't suppose there are some kitty treats in there, too?"

"Sorry, no, just another can of food for you and, sadly, nothing else for me. Not that the food I ate wasn't satisfying, but I suppose my meager wallet will have to pay for the rest of my food on this trip."

"I wouldn't be too sure about that," Onyx said, but when Terra asked him what he meant, he just sighed and curled up on the seat, beginning to snore softly a few moments later.

Probably fake snores. But she had no way to tell, and she'd probably have an answer soon enough anyway. She pulled back onto the road and started off again. If only she had discovered a map packed in the bag along with all that delicious food, because she sure could use one right about now.

Chapter Seven

If Onyx had been asleep, it hadn't been a very deep sleep, because only a few miles later he leapt up and yelled, "Look out!"

Terra slammed on the brakes and swore under her breath, because an old woman was walking across the street who hadn't been there two seconds ago. The woman was wearing a wool coat a few sizes too large for her petite frame, and she was taking her sweet time getting out from in front of Terra's car. But Terra had been reared to have manners, and she'd also been reared to respect her elders, should they not prove to be undeserving of said respect.

She rolled down her window. "Are you lost?" she asked the woman.

The woman shuffled over to Terra's door. "Oh, Lordy, no! You could say I was lost, too, though. Hmm. Maybe if you gave me a ride, I'd figure out which one it was." The woman reached in the window, placing a cool hand on Terra's arm. "Do you think that would be possible, young lady?" Her voice sounded much younger than it should have, and between that fact and her sudden appearance out of nowhere, clearly some sort of magic was afoot.

"I guess I could, as long as you figure out where you're headed soon enough."

"That won't be too hard," the woman told her, and she slowly walked around the car and got into the front seat, where Onyx chose to sit in her lap. "Good kitty," she said, scratching Onyx behind the ear. He began to purr, shoving his head back against her hand. "He wouldn't be *your* familiar, would he, missy?"

"Nope, not that that's any of your business." Terra started the car moving forward again.

"It may be and it may not be. Hard to say at this point."

"She's peculiar," Onyx said softly, turning to look at Terra with wide-open, alert-looking eyes.

"So are you, kitty," the woman said, "but I don't mind if you prefer male cats to female. Can't blame you—I've always preferred them, too." Onyx snorted, but Terra knew he was pleased.

Only a little bit later, the woman began to shout, "Turn left! Turn left! This is it!" She started stomping her feet in excitement. Terra did as she said, swerving off onto a dirt road on the left side of the highway.

They went up a steep, grassy hill, and at the bottom of its other side, Terra saw a large grove of apple trees, all of them covered in bright-red apples. "We're here! Now...let's see... now you just have to find the right apple, Terra!" The woman threw open her door and jumped out, causing Onyx to fall to the ground with a yowl of displeasure. And then, just as suddenly as she'd appeared, she was gone.

"What the hell?" Terra couldn't help being startled. But she might as well take a chance to walk around and stretch, and maybe see if any of these apples seemed extraordinary... or, at least, juicy. She turned off the car and got out, gratefully popping her back and her neck, and then she went around the car to see if Onyx was all right. He'd landed on his feet, but just the same...

"Onyx, you okay?" He had a few flecks of dirt on his face. "You have some—oh!" Onyx had taken off, racing down the path between the trees. Terra didn't think—she just took off after him. She followed his quick little body down the path for about two minutes, passing tree after tree, all of them covered in red apples and bright-green leaves. What on earth was he chasing?

Then the answer became clear, as he scampered up a tree and pinned a small, electric-blue bird between his paw and a branch. "Let me go, you dimwit!" That was the bird, of course. "Let me go or else!"

"Or else what? You'll let me eat you? Why don't you help us out, instead?" Onyx gave the bird a lick, and it shuddered under his tongue.

"You wouldn't want to do that, kitty. You'd get a very bad stomachache if you ate me."

"I very much doubt that," Onyx growled. "Now, is it my lunchtime?"

"No! I'll help you, I will! Just look for the rotten apple, pick it, and you'll find what you need."

"Good birdie." Onyx released it, and it darted off, tweeting angrily as it disappeared through the trees.

"A rotten apple, huh? Of course the one I'm supposed to pick would be inedible. Of course." She caught Onyx with a quiet grunt when he jumped from his high perch. Even magic cats didn't come down from trees easily.

"Look, right up ahead!" he called out.

There it was, at shoulder level—the nastiest-looking apple she had ever seen. A dark, putrid brown, it was crawling with maggots. "Do I really have to pick *that* one?" But it seemed she did, so she shifted Onyx to her left shoulder, then plucked it from the tree as quickly as she could. Once it was in her hand, she fought the strong urge to throw it away and take off in the opposite direction.

But the apple wasn't the same as it had been on the tree. It was now a dark, rich red, the most delicious-looking apple she'd seen in her life. "Talk about opposites." Although she was slightly afraid it would change back mid-chew, she put it to her mouth and took a big bite.

It was every bit as delicious as it had looked—sweet as sugar, and its juices ran straight down her chin. She was only able to enjoy its taste for a moment, though, as next she bit down on something very hard. She yelped, spitting it into her free hand. Amidst the half-chewed bits of apple lay a delicate silver ring. It looked like a wreath of leaves, leaves identical to the ones on the apple trees.

"Put it on."

Terra jumped, almost dropping the ring in the process. The old woman was standing in front of her again, but this time she wore a long, flowing dress, one that, just like the ring, looked just like all the trees' leaves. As the woman slowly walked towards her, Terra realized it was made out of those leaves.

"Put it on?" Terra repeated. "What does it do? Will it turn me into an apple?"

"Oh no, something quite a bit better than that. It will give you the ability to save a life. Your own, or…"

"Or someone else's?" She looked down at the ring again. It seemed to be her size, but just as she was about to put it on her ring finger, she stopped. No, that finger was special—she was saving it. So she put it onto her left middle finger instead, surprised to find that it fit perfectly.

"We're all rooting for you, Terra. Especially your mother." The woman smiled kindly, then looked down at her hand, which seemed to suddenly be holding something. "Oh, and this must be for you," the woman said. "Catch!" She threw whatever it was at Terra, and Terra caught it in the hand that now wore the ring. Looking down, she saw that the woman had thrown a rock at her.

"Hey!" She was about to chew the woman out, but she and Onyx were alone once again. "What an annoying woman, always appearing and disappearing out of nowhere."

"Yes, and I didn't even get to eat that delicious-looking bird."

She placed Onyx on the ground, getting ready to give the rock a closer look. It was flat and oval-shaped, and felt warm against her palm. Turning it over she saw that it said "Doorway" on its other side. "Doorway, huh?"

"Yes, don't you recognize it?" Onyx asked. "It's a doorway stone, of course. Just look for a door and it will take you anywhere you want. All you have to do is place it on the ground in front of the door and go through. And I happen to know that someone is expecting you to do just that, right around now. I'll meet you back at the car." And before she could ask Onyx who he was talking about, or where she would find a door out in the middle of nowhere, he'd taken off, back toward where she'd left the Jaguar.

Terra turned around, planning to follow him and ask him for more information. But instead she shouted, "Fuck!" and took a few quick steps back, holding her now-aching head. Right in front of her stood the door she had been planning to ask Onyx about—a door she'd just slammed her poor head against.

The door was about a foot taller than her and surprisingly familiar looking. Where had she seen it before?

"Of course!" She was delighted, and the headache faded away to nothing almost instantly. She dropped the stone on the ground in front of the door and opened it, walking straight into Athene's bedroom and into her arms.

"How on earth did you..." Before Terra could figure out how to end that sentence, though, Athene kissed her squarely on the lips, and for a few moments, she forgot that she had been about to ask her a question. The kiss was such a good one she almost forgot what the word "question" meant, but when they finally came up for air, she regained her faculties a bit, placing a finger on Athene's lips. "Answers first, sex later."

"I'm not sure my cunt approves of that order, but fine. I suppose I owe you some answers. And I think I know what you're going to ask me, too. Here, come sit down with me." Athene took her hand and led her over to her bed, where they sat down, and Terra listened as Athene began to speak again. "First, the stone is...*was* mine. Now it's yours. I placed a beacon spell on it, in hopes it would find its way to you at the right time, which apparently it has. Second, I didn't tell you because I didn't know if I could actually make the spell work without Onyx's help. Third, yes, I'm willing to have sex with you right now."

Terra chuckled. "My brilliant girlfriend, always thinking ahead. And that third part was kind of obvious, just so you know. But how did you know I would ask?"

"Oh," Athene said, licking her full lips and leaning forward. "Just a hunch." She slipped her burgundy velvet dress over her shoulders and let it fall to the floor, which revealed the fact that she was wearing a strap-on with a *glowing* dildo.

"Why, might I ask, is that dildo glowing, sweetie?" Terra knew she sounded more than a little suspicious, but they'd never used anything during sex that...well...*glowed* before. She knew it wasn't a sign of radioactivity, but a sign of magic. Still, though, what on earth did the glowing mean?

"It's magic, dummy. It's supposed to send warm, orgasmic tingles throughout your body."

Terra reached forward tentatively and touched it lightly with a few fingers. As soon as they met its hard, smooth surface, each woman began to moan—in precise unison, too. "That was... nice." Terra sighed, finding some sort of slight high flittering through her thoughts. A very, very nice high at that. "Mmm, I think I like this dildo. But why did you moan, too?" She turned her curious eyes back up to Athene's face, eagerly waiting for an answer. And, she thought to herself, she was also eagerly waiting for another pulse of pleasure from the dildo.

"Oh, that's just because I can feel everything that touches the dildo." Athene smiled slyly at her, obviously rather proud of herself. "It's kind of like it's my own dick. And look, it has sparkles, too!"

"Yes, it sure does." She grinned. "Damn, Athene, you sure have some good ideas in that lovely head of yours!" Then she made short work of stripping out of her poorly fitting man's dress shirt and slacks. She hadn't bothered to put on anything underneath them, and Athene looked like she was very appreciative of that fact. "It's great to be out of those clothes," Terra said as she removed her feet from the slacks.

"And it's great to *see* you out of them." Athene growled, low and deep, and then leapt at her, grabbing her and tossing her onto the bed. "Get ready to receive the fucking of your life, my little slut."

"Oh, I'm more than ready. Why don't you touch me and see how wet I am?" So incredibly wet, Terra thought to herself as she lay underneath Athene. So incredibly wet, just from touching that amazing, magic dildo.

Athene reached between her legs and gasped as her fingers met Terra's cunt. Yes, she was obviously realizing that Terra had been telling the truth, because she was amazingly, undeniably wet, her pussy more than ready to be entered. But it seemed Athene wasn't ready yet to slide her magical dick inside Terra.

"Why don't you jerk me off a little while I play with your cunt?" she suggested.

"But why can't you…" Terra was desperate to be fucked, but this was worth a try. "I guess I can do that, just for a little while." She reached forward, and instead of saying anything else, she found she had to moan instead as soon as she'd wrapped her hand around Athene's dildo. Her cunt told her loud and clear (or wet and tight) that this had been the right decision.

She began to jerk Athene off, and as she did, Athene slipped two of her fingers inside Terra's dripping cunt. They went in easily, not a single bit of resistance, but Terra was still deliciously tight, her cunt gripping Athene's fingers as they slid in and out of her. Both of them were panting and crying out, and they had only just started. Terra tried to smile as she thought this, but her lips were too busy quivering and letting moan after moan escape.

She was having fun making all kinds of interesting sounds come out of Athene's lips, too, just from sliding her fist up and down the magic dildo. Athene made especially wonderful noises when she added pressure, and even better ones came when she concentrated on the dildo's top, gripping it harder and twisting her fingers around it as she watched Athene make funny, pleasure-filled faces. She knew she was making the same faces, though, as with each movement of her hand, she felt pleasure flowing out of the dildo and into her fingers, traveling down her arm and all the way to her cunt. The pleasure she felt from Athene's touch seemed to be double, if not triple, the usual amount (which was not a small amount of pleasure to begin with).

Terra continued to jerk Athene off, and she almost came the second Athene's fingers traveled to her clit, just barely managing to continue moving her hand up and down the dildo. She held it tighter now, as she gripped and massaged its length, her hold on it as tight as her cunt was around the two fingers thrusting in and out of it. This was her first time jerking off a dildo, though, and definitely her first time with these particular magical powers, so she asked, in between gasps and moans, "How am I doing? Is the speed...the tightness of my fist...does it feel good?"

"Fuck, does it ever! Just keep going, please. I think I'm close...very...very close."

"Me too, Athene, me too." And then, all she could say was, "Oh, Goddess!" because sooner, *much* sooner, than she had expected, her cunt began to squeeze around Athene's fingers, the two fingers that had somehow turned into three, and then, as Athene shoved one last finger inside her, she arched her back and came. Athene just barely managed to put up the magic bubble in time.

And very soon, Terra's sounds began to mingle with those of Athene. As they did, she noticed—with the only bit of brain that wasn't devoted to just feeling pleasure—that the usual sensations of coming were echoing throughout her body in a new, *so* intense way. It was almost too much.

But right before it actually became too much, Terra found her body growing weak, and she collapsed to the bed, panting and more than a little limp-limbed. A few moments later, Athene collapsed at her side.

After only a little while of lying by Athene's side, though, feeling completely spent, Terra popped up. Suddenly, she was full of energy, feeling like she'd just had a double shot of orgasmic espresso. "I feel so...awake and energized all of the sudden."

Then Athene shot up, almost as quickly as Terra had. "Me too! That was part of the spell, as I figured that after feeling that much pleasure, we might need a little recharge."

"Great thinking, honey," she said with a quick kiss on Athene's nose, "like always."

"We both know that neither of us is exactly an idiot."

"That's for sure! Especially me, when it comes to choosing who to fall in love with. I picked a real winner in you, you know." Then Terra remembered something. "The woman in the orchard...she said something about my mom...what was it?" She chewed at her lip for a moment, then raised her hand, pointing her finger at the ceiling. "Aha! It *was* about my mom. She said something like...'We're all rooting for you, especially your mom.' Yeah, that was it. What the heck do you think she meant, Athene?"

"Your mom? And 'We're all'...all of some kind of group...I can't say I understand, really, but maybe this means you'll get to see your mom."

"Don't say that, don't. It's too sad." Terra had thought she'd seen her a few times, reflected in mirrors and on shiny surfaces, but that was when she was a bit younger, and she had always believed she'd just imagined those sightings. She'd dreamed about her mother a number of times too, also when she was younger, and they had been good dreams, but she'd known it wasn't really her mom in them...or was that still true?

"I used to dream about her, you know." She wasn't looking at Athene when she said this, but instead was staring out the bedroom's large window, only barely taking in the redwood trees at the edge of the Werths' land. "It happened on and off for a number of years. From when I was about fourteen to when I was sixteen or so. She was always telling me something... something about how I had more power than I realized, and that I would begin to receive it when I was older, or whatever. But they were all just dreams."

"Or they were visions." Terra whipped her head back toward Athene, and Athene sighed. "Or they were nothing. Who knows?" she said, putting up her hands in a sign of defeat. "I'm almost positive you'll know someday. I may not have the ability to predict the future, but I think Onyx might, just a little, so maybe he can help you with this once you go back through the door to wherever you were before."

"I don't think I'm going to ask him. It's obviously just nonsense." But when she saw the hurt look on Athene's face, she sighed and reached toward her, brushing a few hairs from her slightly sweaty face and tucking them back behind her ear. "Now, do you have any clothes I can borrow? I doubt I'll run into anyone in the orchard, but just in case…"

Chapter Eight

Once Terra was properly dressed again, in a pale-pink T-shirt and women's jeans, she went back through the door, blowing Athene a kiss as she stepped through it and back into the apple orchard. She started to head back toward her car, the "doorway" rock in one of her jeans' tiny pockets. She'd have to be extra careful with it, as she really didn't want to lose her only way to see Athene during this journey. Yes, this was an excellent turn of events, the fact that she could still see Athene—still see her and still have amazing sex with her, too. But of course, she thought with a smile, that was only a faraway second to being in Athene's arms, fully clothed, and feeling the love in the way Athene held her so, so tight.

Soon, she was back to the Jaguar, and back to Onyx as well, who was lying on his side on the car's hood, looking like he might slide off it at any moment. He slowly lifted his head as Terra reached him. "Ah, the simple pleasure of a warm car and a warm sun. A shame you humans can't enjoy such things as well as us cats."

"And it's a shame 'we humans' are much bigger than you cats, too," Terra said, and she grabbed him off the car's hood and swung him back and forth a few times.

"You win, you bitch! Now put me down."

"'Put me down' what?"

"Please?"

She did as he requested, placing him on the dirt, and then she opened her car door, waiting a moment so he could get in first. Once he had settled into his now-official spot, she got into the car and started it.

"Have fuuun?" he asked in a devilish tone.

"Oh, shut up." She rubbed his head and then began to turn the car around. "And yes. More than you can imagine."

"Hey, it's not my fault there aren't any other gay cats on the grounds. You don't have to rub it in."

"Sorry, kitty. I'll look into that when we get back. After all, I'll owe you one. Or two. I already do!"

"Thank you," Onyx said, and he actually sounded like he meant it. Terra couldn't imagine going without sex for as long as he must have, but then she grimaced at the thought. She really, really didn't want to be thinking about a cat's sex life, or even its lack thereof.

They got back onto the highway and started heading in the same direction as before. Terra was happy that it was a beautiful day where they were, wherever the hell that happened to be. Meeting that woman and getting the ring seemed to be a good sign, though, and so did the fact that she was now happily sated sexually, at least for the time being. Right before she'd left, Athene had told her to come again (hopefully in more than one way!) that day's night, sometime after nine p.m. She hoped she would have found somewhere to stay by then, because it was starting to seem like this middle-of-nowhere business she was currently experiencing might last for a long, long time.

But after about two hours of driving, and shortly after cresting a steep hill, she could see what looked like a midsized town only a few miles down the road. They soon passed a sign that read MISSIOU TOWN LIMITS.

"Wonderful!" Terra exclaimed.

Onyx stopped snoring as she did so, shaking his head back and forth. "What is it? Are we there yet?" he asked sleepily.

"Wherever 'there' is, yeah. Apparently we're almost to Missiou City. Or just Missiou, I guess. Ever heard of it?"

"Sounds...vaguely familiar."

"You sound vaguely familiar, too."

"Ha. Ha. Hopefully, once I'm done laughing, we'll be there, and I can get a nice room to sleep in. I was starting to worry I'd be stuck on this lumpy car seat for the whole night."

"Lumpy? This car is a classic, in perfect condition, and I happen to think the seats are rather comfortable."

He scoffed. "You humans have no idea what true comfort is. None at all." Onyx jumped forward and placed his front paws on the dashboard, stretching out to his full length. "Civilization at last. At least I *suppose* you could call it that."

"Your standards are too high," Terra said, as they pulled into the city and onto what was apparently Main Street. "I think it's delightfully...quaint."

The buildings were all one-story high, it seemed, with wooden, retro-style signs in front of the storefronts. They passed a couple of barbershops, both with the old-fashioned spinning barber's poles in front of them, and a number of clothing stores and a drugstore. A few minutes later, Terra noticed a parking spot in front of a restaurant that appeared to be open. Painted on the large window, in dark-green lettering, were the words THE TOWN RESTAURANT, a name she couldn't help chuckling at. Beneath the silly name, it said something much less funny— LUNCH FROM 12-2. It was much less funny because, having eaten breakfast close to six and a half hours ago, she was a fair bit beyond merely being hungry. "I'll make sure to get something with meat in it," she told Onyx as she pulled into the parking spot. "So you don't feel as bad about having to wait in the car."

"You mean I have to wait? And without a magazine to read?"

"Didn't think to pack one, sorry."

Onyx sighed loudly, then settled down onto the seat and crossed his paws. "Something with chicken, if you please."

She parked and got out, after making sure to roll down the windows a few inches so it wouldn't become too hot for Onyx. It wasn't especially hot outside the car, but it was rather warm—pleasantly warm, with a slight breeze tossing her short hair just a little as she walked toward the restaurant's front door.

Once inside, she found a table and waited to be noticed. A few moments later, a waitress with lustrous red hair and a tiny black apron came over to where she was sitting, handing her a laminated menu and giving her a big grin. "Want something to drink, honey? We have the best sweet tea you've ever had, since our chef comes from the South."

That was at least one hint about her and Onyx's whereabouts. They weren't in the South, whatever the South was. But it seemed to be the one Terra knew about, since she knew sweet tea was usually served in the southern United States. Did that mean she was still *in* the United States? She decided it was probably not smart to ask, lest she sound like a loony. Probably not a good idea to ask if there was any magic in this town, either. Instead, she told the waitress, "Sweet tea sounds great. And does the menu have anything with chicken in it?"

"We have a very yummy chicken-salad sandwich. Comes with coleslaw or fries."

"I'll have the coleslaw."

"Be right back with your sweet tea, then, hon."

She couldn't help watching the waitress as she walked away. Her face had been quite cute, but her sashaying butt created a few fantasies of said butt and what it might feel like cupped in Terra's hands. Athene was much more attractive, but both of them still found other people attractive, too, and neither of them really wanted to become members of the "thought police." They'd even turned each other on a few times with stories about what a threesome would be like, but neither of them wanted it to go beyond that.

She might have liked that waitress's cute, tight butt, but she didn't love it, much less love her. That fact, though, didn't manage to stop a bit of fantasizing from flitting through her head as she waited for the waitress to return.

When the redhead returned with her tea, Terra had to resist the strong urge to shake her head a little in order to clear out the last fragments of her short fantasy.

She gave the waitress a small smile and thanked her. Because she was starting to blush a little, she turned her head away, busying herself with pulling the paper off her glass's straw. Then she realized something. "Any chance I could get some water in a to-go cup? My cat's waiting in the car, and I'd love to take him some, as I didn't realize today would be so warm. He'll chew me out if I don't."

Terra almost clapped her hand over her mouth, but the waitress just laughed. "Sure thing. I can even bring it to you in a soup to-go bowl. Be right back."

After she returned with the water, Terra took it out to Onyx, who looked both surprised and pleased when he saw the bowl. "You know I don't have to drink and eat as often as a normal cat, but I was getting a touch thirsty in this warm weather. What a dear girl you are." She placed it on the floor in front of his seat, and he climbed down to it, beginning to lap away. He was purring when she left him, which made her feel like it had been worth the little bit of extra effort.

Terra almost started purring herself once she was back inside, as an incredibly delicious-looking sandwich sat on a checkered plate next to a small bowl of purple-and-green coleslaw. The first bite was just as good as she'd guessed it would be, and she devoured two-thirds of the sandwich in almost no time at all. Two-thirds, because she was saving the last third for Onyx. If he had been that grateful for the water, she couldn't wait to see his reaction to the sandwich.

And Onyx was indeed delighted, gobbling up the meat and bread in no time at all. Terra had already removed the remaining lettuce and tomato, but she hadn't expected him to lick up the bit of coleslaw that had wound up in the box as well.

"I didn't know cats liked coleslaw," Terra told him as she watched him devour the last bites of food.

"Mrrmph, mmm, crmnph. No, *cats* usually don't. But really, darling, do you think I am just a mere little pussy cat?"

"Of course not, Onyx. You're much cuter than a normal cat, for one thing."

"While I appreciate a compliment just as much as the next fellow, I must stop you there and begin to groom myself. That sandwich proved to be a rather messy endeavor." Onyx licked his paw and rubbed it across his face once, then a second time. Her work on the kitty's behalf was done, at least for the time being, so why not take in the town while the weather remained nice? After all, she had a fair number of hours before she wanted to turn in, and she wanted them to pass quickly, as right before she slept for the night, she would be visiting Athene with the special rock. So she shut and locked her door, and started exploring.

As she had said to Onyx, the town sure was "quaint." Terra didn't know if it was intentional or just that they were low on money for updating things. But after seeing a few SHOPPEs and GENERAL STOREs, she decided that yes, they were going for retro and probably hoping it would draw in tourists. That was a title she qualified for, she realized, and for the first time ever, too.

She hadn't had enough time off from working in the mansion to take in the sights anywhere other than the city it was on the outskirts of. The mansion and its grounds weren't short on beauty or entertainment, so she hadn't really considered what she was missing. Not until now. Being somewhere she'd never been before, which hadn't happened since she was fourteen, was kind of nice. Refreshing, even, perhaps. She enjoyed noticing all the differences from where she lived—how the people were dressed, what the center of the town looked like. Everything was delightfully different and new.

And then something less different caught her eye, in the form of a store across the street. She gasped as she read the dark-windowed store's hanging sign: YE OLDE MAGICK SHOPPE—ENTER IF YE DARE.

Well, did she dare? Hell yeah, she did, so she dashed across the street, causing a few honks and one "Ma'am, please watch where you're going," which came from a man in a red truck. Now that was more than a little different, too. Who was ever that polite in *her* city?

Once she was safely across the street, thankfully without causing any accidents, she saw an OPEN sign hanging from a hook on the shop's wooden front door, a door that was also open itself, but just a few inches. A glass ball sitting on a metal stand was holding it that way, so she stepped over both carefully as she swung open the door and walked inside.

But Terra had always been a little accident-prone, and so she was only a little surprised when her foot caught on the ball and sent it rolling across the floor. It rolled until it reached the feet of a skinny, short man, who had a balding head of wild, white hair and, seemingly, very quick reflexes, as he caught the ball while walking toward Terra. Standing up, he cupped it in his hand, staring down at it for a moment. "If only I'd been given the full gift of divination like my mother. But all I have is her leftover wine cellar, and with its bottles so heavily depleted—I do fancy a good glass of wine from time to time—I can't be sure if you're Terra or someone else." He looked up from the ball now and placed it on a mid-height shelf at his shoulder level. Strangely, the perfectly round ball stayed in place, even though gravity would normally have dictated otherwise.

But she was clearly in the world of magic again, and the normal laws of science were only occasionally welcome in that realm. "May I ask you what your name is, before I tell you whether I'm Terra?"

"Just like her mother, quick on her feet. Hmm, what do you think?" He was silent for a few moments, then straightened his horn-rimmed glasses. "Yes, I suppose you're right."

"You must be Terra," he said, walking over to her and extending his hand, "and I am Jeremy. My people don't do what your people do and act grandiose when we name our children. No, we prefer to lead a simple life, except when there are Wolfrans in the backs of our shops. And she's been there for years, hasn't she?"

Terra had been ready to shake Jeremy's hand, ready to do that and then ask him how he knew her mother (it seemed everyone so far had known her, actually). But he had withdrawn his hand just as she'd reached for it, and so instead she placed her hand on her hip as she asked him, "So what's this business with a...Wolfran, or whatever?"

"Ah, the glorious, deadly Wolfran. You know, my dear, this used to be a two-person shop, run by me and my brother Mason. But our pleasant times together were not ended by a normal death, no sir. They were ended by a Wolfran moving into the cave behind our store. Now, if you'll just follow me..." Jeremy turned and began walking toward what must have been the sales counter, as an outdated-looking cash register sat on it next to an opening that Jeremy was now walking through.

"Wait a minute, Jeremy." Now she had both hands on her hips. "Wait just one minute. I didn't agree to help, you know," she said, following him as quickly as she could. For a man who must have been less than five feet tall, he really could move! "I don't even know if I can trust you." Now she followed him through a beaded curtain behind the counter. "I don't even know if…"

On the other side of the curtain, it was twilight, and she was standing a few feet away from a large cave's opening, suddenly waist deep in dry, sweet-smelling grass, and possibly waist deep in trouble, too. "What happened?" she called out. "Where the hell am I? Jeremy, or whoever the hell you are—what have you done?"

"Merely what I said I was going to, and just what Mason told me to. Don't worry, you will be rewarded. Look in the mouth of the cave for your weapon." He was standing behind her now, but just as she started toward him, he pushed back through the beaded curtain and was gone. Terra rushed up to the curtain and flung it back, but the only thing behind it was more grass and more twilight. "I'll let you come back once you've vanquished the beast!" Jeremy's voice now seemed to be coming from very far away.

And it also "seemed" that she was mightily pissed. She didn't have much of a choice, though, so, with a fair bit of fear, she went up to the cave's entrance and looked inside. "Holy mother!" she gasped, clapping her hand over her mouth. At least four human skeletons littered the floor, and there was another one that looked like it might have been part something else. So, she was supposed to go up against some beast that had killed this many people? Just to return to her quest?

Or perhaps this was *part* of her quest. Could that be it? "Vanquish a foe," as Zeus had said the previous night. "Huh, worth a try," and she glanced around for any sort of weapon. Off to her right, a few feet inside the cave, she saw a glint of silver. Anything would do at this point, so she went over to it to check it out. It turned out to be a foot-long, unsheathed dagger, with runes or something similar to them carved into the blade. It was this or nothing, because it was the only weapon she could see in there. Unless she wanted to use someone's femur.

She began to go farther inside the cave. Luckily, a fair bit of light was coming in through cracks and holes in its roof and walls. A few steps deeper in, she heard a sound of some sort. That wasn't a...*roar*, was it? She began to shake a little, but told herself it was just because it was cold in here, and not because she was scared shitless.

Then, "That was *definitely* a roar!" she gasped, as a large, scary rumble echoed throughout the tunnel she was in. Either bravely (or stupidly), she still kept walking, deeper and deeper inside, until she reached a large opening. And there stood the creature the sounds were coming from, a creature that whipped its giant head toward her and bared its far-too-large teeth in a growl.

The Wolfran looked like a wolf, so the name made sense. But unlike a normal wolf, it had large, dark-brown wings, and its head was about the size of her torso. She held up the dagger and assumed what she hoped was a good fighting stance. "I have come to kill you!" she cried out.

But instead of getting ready to attack, the Wolfran seemed almost to smile. It walked over to her, and instead of biting off her head, it gave her face a big, juicy lick. "A woman! At last, I have fellow female company!" It—or, as Terra realized now, she—nuzzled Terra's face, then sat down in front of her and lay down. "You can't imagine what it's been like, seeing man after man come through here. All wanting to kill me, like you. But you won't fail, I promise."

"And why...why won't I? I'm no match for you, Wolfran."

"Call me Katherine, dear. And I'll lay it out for you. I want to die, so I can be sent to our creatures' heaven, our paradise.

I've lived for too long and seen too much, and to be honest, dear, I'm just plumb tuckered out. The story is this: my dear, dear husband, Gabriel, was killed by a man, so I vowed, as I watched him die, that no man would ever manage to do the same to me. But you are clearly not a man, and so it is my wish that you take my life. I beg of you, do it quickly."

"I can't kill you, Katherine!" How on earth could she kill a kindly seeming creature she'd only just met? Terra was staring at the Wolfran's face as she spoke, so she didn't notice when the dagger began to glow or as it began to rise toward Katherine's chest. When she did notice, she shrieked and tried to pull it back, back and away from the Wolfran. But it just drew closer and closer, the pull of it too strong for Terra to fight off, until, with one strong jerk forward, the whole length of it sank into the right side of Katherine's chest.

Terra began to cry then and watched with tear-filled eyes as the Wolfran's body began to fade, more and more, until only a blue, ghostly outline remained. Then an image appeared behind Katherine, an image that looked like a meadow full of spring flowers. The Wolfran turned her large blue head, and Terra heard her say, so very softly, "My sweet, sweet wolf, I'm coming to you now, finally."

The last thing she heard her say before Katherine walked away was, "Thank you. This fulfills the first part of your quest, although I swear I am no longer anyone's foe, least of all yours."

Before Terra could get a closer look at the fields Katherine had entered, she heard a small clicking sound and watched as, far too quickly, the fields, the flowers, and then, last of all, Katherine disappeared. She was almost certain, though, that she saw another winged wolf running up to the female Wolfran just as the door to the flower-filled paradise closed.

Chapter Nine

Outside the cave, the beaded curtain was still there. Feeling somewhat emotionally exhausted, Terra walked up to it and pulled back the beads. There was the shop, and there stood Jeremy, holding a dusty bottle of what must have been wine in his right hand.

"Looks like you were right, my brother!" he shouted toward the ceiling. Then Jeremy looked at Terra. "He thought she had something against men, you see, and so—"

"You fucking *bastard*!" Terra shoved him against the counter. Then she stepped back from him and sighed, wiping the last few tears from her face with the back of her hand. "I guess you didn't have the whole story."

"We men never do with you womenfolk. Was she nice to you, then?"

"Far too nice to someone who took her life. Not that she was wishing for anything else from me, but still…"

"Ah, I seem to have misjudged the Wolfran. Your brother gets killed by a beast—a creature, I mean—and you just can't look at it in a level-headed way. My brother kept telling me to just wait till the quest began and someone named Terra arrived. Then our wolf problem would go away. He also liked my mother's wine, you see, and that's how he could tell you were coming. He knew you could help us, but then it was just me, and he kept trying to convince me I was looking at things all cockeyed. Then again, he was always trying to convince me of that, old jerkface. Well, here, young woman. You've more than earned this." He held out the dusty wine bottle and Terra took it from him. It felt heavier than she'd expected, much heavier, so she wobbled a little once he wasn't holding onto it any longer.

"Drink it all in one sitting, preferably when you won't be driving anywhere. It will give you a vision of your future, and I hope for your sake it's a good one. I'm closing for the day now, though, got a lot of filing and the like to do. Thank you again, and you can show yourself out."

What a strange, and rather rude, man, Terra thought as she left. And what a sweet, lovely creature Katherine seemed to be. She glanced back at the store once more right before she crossed the street, but the store's sign was different now. No longer saying YE OLDE MAGICK SHOPPE, it now stated that the store was for rent and listed a number to call for inquiries.

Admittedly, that didn't surprise her much. This magic stuff, all of these experiences outside of the Werths' mansion and its surrounding city, well, she just might be starting to get used to it. Which would hopefully pay off in the long run.

Back at the car, Onyx asked her why she'd been gone so long. It was only then she realized it was now dusk and, according to her watch, almost five hours after she had finished lunch. "I was...helping someone," she told him, and refused to tell him any more, no matter how many questions he asked after they began to drive down Main Street. "All I'm willing to tell you is that we need to find somewhere to stay for the night, although I don't know how affordable it'll be."

"Check your wallet when we get there. You should have somewhere around eight hundred dollars in it, if I'm remembering correctly."

"Well, damn! How sweet of Athene…unless *you* put it there, Onyx."

Onyx shook his head, and Terra smiled, thinking about the fact that her lunch had cost about eight dollars. That was an *extremely* large one-hundredth of what Athene had given her, she thought with a chuckle.

"What's so funny, doll?" Onyx glared up at her with narrowed eyes. "Are you laughing at the sorry state of my fur coat? Sitting in this car all day didn't exactly do wonders for my looks, you know."

"No, you're perfectly pulled together, as usual, Onyx. I'm just…it's just…never mind. Hey, check it out, there's an inn right up ahead!"

Its sign read, Raven's Inn and Restaurant. Good, she could probably have dinner there, too. She still had one can of cat food left for Onyx, but she couldn't eat it with him, of course. Hopefully the restaurant would have decent food.

Inside the inn's front door stood an absolutely beautiful desk, with graceful-seeming mermaids as well as waves and seashells carved into its legs. On top of it were some papers and a shiny brass bell, which Terra rang. A voluptuous woman wearing a low-cut T-shirt and a heather-gray pencil skirt came from around a corner behind the desk. "Oh, hello there! Were you hoping to get a room for the night?"

"Yes, I was. How much would your cheapest room be?"

"Actually, we're completely vacant right now, so I can give you our nicest room at a great bargain: eighty including room tax, plus you get a ten-dollar coupon for our restaurant. The clam chowder there is to die for, totally delish. How does that sound?"

"Great. Especially the clam chowder."

The woman giggled, then got a key off the wall behind the desk. "You'll be in room eight. Now, will you be paying with credit?"

"Nope, cash. One thing, first, though. Do you allow pets?"

"Do we allow pets? Ha!" The woman whistled, and moments later, three Shih Tzus tore down the hall to Terra's left and dashed behind the counter, yipping happily. "What's your pet's name?"

"Onyx, and he's a cat."

"Oh, my dogs love kitties. Maybe they can play together."

Terra almost grimaced at the thought. Onyx was a bit of an elitist when it came to dogs, believing they'd only been put on this earth to make cats look better. "He doesn't really feel safe around dogs, I'm afraid, no matter how nice they are to him."

"Well, I'll make sure Frank, Dean, and Sammy Junior are in the back when you bring him through. Will he be needing dinner too? Our chef, my husband, will be happy to make Onyx something to sup on. Sandy makes a lovely dish he calls Catty Catfish, and we happen to have some fresh from our nearby bay, just in this afternoon."

"That would be lovely. Thanks...what's your name?"

"Oh!" The woman clasped her hand to her chest. "Silly me. I'm Raven, Raven Thick. A pleasure to meet you. And you are?"

"It's Terra." The woman took her hand, but instead of shaking it, she brought it to her lips and gave it a loud kiss.

"Well, young lady, go ahead and bring your stuff in, and your darling kitty, and we'll settle the bill."

"Be right back," Terra told her, walking out the building's front door. That woman's a bit of a character, she thought to herself, but a likeable one, for sure. It was nice that Raven was so fond of animals, too, a trait Terra had always appreciated in Magic Ones and humans alike. It was a trait her father and her mother had shared.

She told Onyx about the inn and warned him about the dogs. "I don't think they'll be out and about when we go in, though."

"Thank *God*. You know how I despise those insipid ruffians you people call 'dogs.'"

Terra got her bag out of the car and locked it, and Onyx followed her inside the inn. She paid Raven while the innkeeper gave Onyx some attention, and soon he was purring loudly. He continued to purr as they walked down the hall and went into their room, where, once inside, Terra thought she also should start purring.

The walls were covered in elegant, pale-blue fleur-de-lis wallpaper, and the bed had one large fleur-de-lis on its incredibly thick comforter. A large, claw-footed tub sat to the left of the bed, with gold feet and faucet, and some towels lay beside it that were some of the softest she had ever felt, as she discovered midway through exploring the room. A bidet in the bathroom stood opposite the toilet, and the sink had a blue-and-gold-flecked marble top, with expensive-looking toiletries to its left. A large, glass-enclosed shower stall completed the bathroom's perfection.

She was desperate to take a shower, partially because it had been awhile since she'd bathed, and partially because the shower had one of those removable showerheads. The water pressure in a place this fancy would probably be ideal for particular things, like getting a specific area of her body squeaky clean, to begin with. She grabbed the shampoo, the conditioner, and the soap from the sink's counter, and then shut and locked the bathroom door after telling Onyx she was going to take a quick shower. Locking the door wasn't exactly necessary, as Onyx was a little short on thumbs and wouldn't be able to operate the doorknob. But he had a fair bit of magical power buried beneath all that fur, so she figured the click of the lock would be a good-enough indication that she wanted privacy.

Once the water was the right temperature, she got under the showerhead and sighed, low and deep. Yes, this would do nicely. She washed her body first, teasing herself a little with the occasional splash of water on her mons pubis. Then, once her hair and body were clean, it was time for some fun. She inched the showerhead lower and lower, first over each of her breasts, then down her stomach, until she finally reached her cunt. The water shooting out of the showerhead was exactly where it belonged—hitting her clit good and hard.

Now it was time to add a little more to the experience. Terra pictured Athene wearing a white satin bra and matching panties. In her fantasy, Athene was starting to walk toward her, and Terra was sitting in a chair, her wrists bound behind it. Athene climbed into her lap, facing her, and slowly dragged her fingers across Terra's face. Then she brought back her hand and slapped her, good and hard, across her left cheek. In her fantasy, she jumped from the impact, but her body flushed with heat from it as well. Her body was flushed with heat in the shower, too, both from the hot water shooting onto her clit and from the dirty thoughts in her head.

Next, Athene bent forward, her lips inches away from Terra's, and cupped Terra's cunt with a hot, firm hand. She leaned back and moved into a position with more space between the two of them, and then she climbed off Terra, and, both in her fantasy and in reality, Terra gasped.

Her fantasy version of Athene stood behind her next, and it was her cunt, and not her cheek, that got a hard smack. Terra almost jumped from the impact in the shower, the fantasy seemed so real. Athene gave her pussy a few good hard smacks, each one making Terra writhe around as much as her constraints allowed. Then Athene untied her, led her over to the bed, and slid her hand into Terra's panties and began to play with her. Every time she got close, Athene would stop and bite her—a bite on her arm, one on her side, one on her neck. And in between each bite came more pleasure from Athene's skilled hand, her hand's touches and caresses replicated by the showerhead held in Terra's actual hand. And while Terra was being tortured and teased in her fantasy, in reality she was getting closer and closer, too. It almost felt like Athene's hand was touching her instead of the steady beat of the water, because showerheads didn't normally feel that good (and Terra had gotten lots and *lots* of experience with them during her dry spells). She kept picturing Athene touching her, teasing her, pleasuring her, until it was just too much, and she came—hard—and collapsed against the shower's back wall.

She took a few moments to catch her breath, panting a little from the orgasm, and then she looked down at her arm, because she noticed it seemed to be hurting a little. There, right near her shoulder, were slight indentations—*tooth marks*.

"What the hell?" Apparently, the fantasy Athene had come into reality a bit, it seemed. Was this...had she done this? Well, she wasn't about to start complaining, because it had been the best fantasy sex of her life. It still didn't measure up to the real thing, but it had done the trick for the time being—for the space between that moment and when she might next see Athene in the flesh.

She finished her shower and got out, using the bathroom's hairdryer and her fingers to style her hair as best as she could without a brush. Of course, she hadn't thought to bring one, as all she had brought was her wallet (now full of Athene's money) and the clothes she was planning to wear to dinner this night. Hopefully the restaurant wouldn't turn her away, although the slacks and shirt she had packed were nice enough. She didn't really have anything at all in her full wardrobe that was especially fancy. After all, what use did a maid have for gowns and the like?

Back in her sitting room, she sat down on a plush, dark-brown armchair and put her legs up on its stool. Onyx jumped into her lap and started purring.

"Feel like you're in the lap of luxury, Onyx?"

"Har-dy-har-har. But yes, this room is quite to my liking. If they have anything at the restaurant that is fit for felines, I will be completely satisfied, but until then—"

"Raven, the innkeeper, said they have a catfish dish they make exclusively for cats, and that the catfish they'd be using just came in this afternoon."

"Oh, my goodness!" Onyx's purrs became even louder, and he leapt off Terra's lap. "Well, don't dilly-dally, my dear. I will anxiously look forward to your return." He nudged her legs off the footstool with his nose, then pushed against her calves after she stood up, guiding her toward the room's door.

"Hmm, you're being subtle for once, my little kitty friend. I get it—you want to have catfish. I'll be back soon."

"You do that," Onyx said as she shut the door.

She went to the front desk to ask Raven how to get to the restaurant. "Go out our front door and to the right. You'll see the restaurant's entrance right away, two double doors with round, stained-glass windows. Oh! I almost forget." The innkeeper reached into a drawer in her desk and handed Terra a piece of paper. "Here's your coupon. Give it to them along with your payment when you get the bill. Enjoy your dinner!"

"Thanks, Raven."

The restaurant was right down from the inn's front door, just like Raven had said. A male maitre d' with slicked-back blond hair and a lovely, sonorous voice led her to a table and told her that her waiter would be right over. A few moments later, she was brought a menu and a small basket of bread, which was flecked with rosemary and, she discovered with her first bite, absolutely divine. She did as Raven had suggested and ordered a bowl of clam chowder, as well as a to-go box of the Catty Catfish.

After she'd ordered, a glass of white wine somehow found its way to her table, despite the fact that she hadn't ordered one.

"Compliments of the gentleman over in the corner," the waiter told her, but when she looked, no one was there. She decided to stay on the side of caution, so she didn't touch the wine, instead telling the waiter that she didn't drink.

She was more than happy to dig into the clam chowder, though, which was rich, creamy, and, well, *perfect*. She finished it much faster than she would have liked to, and then the bill came. Terra picked up the paper and saw that it came to around eighteen dollars. Too bad it didn't come to ten instead, she thought.

But then the paper began to shake a little, and when it stopped, the total instead said ten dollars, even. That might have been incredibly convenient, but it still managed to startle her. She hadn't done that, had she? No way could she change it back now, even if it had been her doing, so she gave the waiter her coupon and a fifteen-dollar tip, which she hoped would help to offset her guilt at the total shrinking by so much.

She was a little shaken as she returned to her room, and Onyx noticed instantly. "You okay, sweetkins?"

"Oh, yeah. Just…something strange happened back at the restaurant. Two somethings, actually." She told him about the free wine from the invisible man, and then she told him about the seemingly magical event with her bill.

"Three things. First, I think it was very smart of you to not touch that wine. One of your competitors might have found you out, and he might have done something to that drink. That's my guess, at least. Second, I don't know what changed the bill, but who knows—it really could have been you."

"And third?" she asked him, placing the box of Catty Catfish on the floor and popping it open.

"I was going to ask you what that heavenly scent was, but now I know." He raced over to the patty of fish and began to attack it, loudly and with a lot of *mmms* and what almost sounded like growls.

After he'd finished it and had licked the box completely clean—in what must have only been about a minute—he burped loudly and hopped onto the bed, licking his chops a few times. "Oh. My. God. That was one of the most delicious things I have ever tasted in my life. Thank you, Terra, and my compliments to the chef, as well. I'd almost give my firstborn to him in thanks."

"You're never going to have a firstborn, Onyx."

"Nor do I want one, of course. I suppose it would be an empty promise."

Terra took off her slacks and shirt and placed them on the bed; she thought her girlfriend might appreciate her arriving in only panties and a bra. She sat on the bed for a few minutes, then looked at the hotel room's bedside clock. It was now five after nine, right when she was supposed to visit her sweetie. She went over to Athene's jeans and took the doorway rock out of the right pocket, then placed it in front of her room's door. "Let's hope it works this time," she said, turning toward Onyx, "because otherwise I'm about to walk into the inn's hallway in nothing but my underwear."

It did work, though, and instantly, she was in the room of Athene, who grinned lasciviously at her lack of clothing. "Nice panties, and nice tits, too. But do you want to talk about your quest so far, at least a little first, perhaps? I have to admit, I'm dying to know what you've been up to all day long."

Athene didn't look half bad to Terra, either, dressed in a short, body-skimming nightgown made of pink lace and nothing else. She could see Athene's nipples through the fabric, but despite the wetness their sight brought to a now *very* happy part of her body, she did think Athene deserved to know what she'd accomplished so far.

She sat next to Athene on the room's lavender-and-cream checkered couch and began with the most important part. "I've already vanquished the foe," she told Athene with a proud grin.

"The foe? What do you mean?"

"Oh! I guess you don't know what Zeus—or whoever was speaking at the time—told us." She proceeded to share his words with Athene, and then continued with what had happened in Missiou so far, all about Jeremy and the cave. She got a little choked up as she talked about Katherine, and Athene seemed to notice, placing a gentle hand over Terra's and squeezing it.

She decided against telling Athene about the wine and the disappearing man who had sent it to her, but she did mention the part about her check changing.

"Wow! You know, I may be wrong, but I think it *was* you. I mean, you do have a touch of magic in you, even if it isn't a lot. Maybe this quest is giving you more, too…or, maybe, it's bringing out the magic that was already there."

"Who the heck knows? I know one thing for sure, though," she said, and leaned much closer to Athene and lowered her voice. "I know for sure…absolutely…without a single fucking doubt in my mind…that I want you. Right now. *Intensely.*"

"The feeling is more than mutual," Athene told her with a small, mischievous smile, and then both of them stopped speaking for the time being, as their lips met and talking became impossible…and unnecessary.

They kissed as their hands worked like mad to strip themselves—and each other—of their clothing. It didn't take long at all before they were on the bed and entangled, both of them completely naked. They had resumed kissing, and Terra found she loved the tentativeness of Athene's kisses; as she kissed her back, Terra silently hoped that Athene was enjoying the much more ravenous kisses she gave her in return.

"I have an idea," Terra said to Athene when they finally let their lips part (a slightly unpleasant and possibly ill-advised action). "As unhappy as interrupting our kissing makes me," and Athene laughed and stroked Terra's arm, "I thought of something. Why don't you loan me your strap-on? I want to try it out…I want to feel what you were feeling the other day," she said, reaching between Athene's thighs and sliding her fingers down, beginning to gently tease her hole with her fingertips. "I want to feel what it's like to fuck a woman, to slide my *dick* inside her hole." Terra punctuated the word "dick" by entering Athene with a couple of her fingers, and Athene moaned out a "Yes, please," as Terra began to fuck her.

"It's in…my beds—*fuck*…my bedside table," Athene stuttered out as Terra, wicked girl that she was, decided to fill her slicked-up hole with a third finger.

It was almost painful to remove her fingers, then, but she felt close to desperate to find out what it felt like to be inside a woman, what it felt like to be inside *her* woman. So Terra opened the bedside table's drawer and reached inside, taking out the strap-on. It wasn't glowing when she first set eyes on it, but it began to emit light when she picked it up, growing even brighter when she pulled the straps over her legs and thighs and cinched them up. "What, it doesn't adjust itself?" she joked, and then she gasped as the straps tightened a little around her body, inching up bit by bit until it seemed to be adjusted completely perfectly. "Wow. That was kinda…weird."

"Yeah, it was." Athene's eyes were now locked onto the strap-on. She didn't look nervous, though, just curious. "It never did that for me, actually," she said.

It had been startling, Terra thought, but it was cool, too, and besides, she'd put on the strap-on for a reason. "Too much talking, too little fucking," she proclaimed, and she flipped Athene onto her stomach and grabbed her hips, pulling her ass up into the air. As she began to enter Athene's pussy with the dildo, she was amazed that she could feel the dildo sliding inside— so that was what men felt, was it? She took in the tightness of her girlfriend's hole, the wetness of it, too, and the equally wonderful feeling of Athene's cunt gripping the dildo, so, so tight. And then there was the friction, of course, as she began to pump in and out of her. It made her gasp, because it was, in a word, *incredible*. No, that wasn't enough...*miraculous*? *Astounding*? No, that word didn't manage to sum it up, either. She'd just have to invent a new one.

Athene seemed to think it was pretty terrific too, because she was writhing around beneath her, shoving her ass against Terra's incredibly sensitive dildo every minute or two. Terra couldn't help laughing a little as she continued to fuck her lover. It just felt so, so good!

"What's so...oh!...funny?"

"Nothing," Terra said, still laughing a little. It's just," *giggle, giggle*, "it's just that, um...ha! Just that this is the most fucking just...*amazariffictastic* thing I've ever felt. That's all. Oh, God!"

"That's all? And I don't think that's a...oh, God!...word, you know." Athene laughed now, too, but soon they both stopped laughing, because all the lovely sensations the dildo was causing seemed to be escalating in intensity. They totally were for Terra, and she could tell from Athene's sounds and her body's movements that she seemed to be feeling just as good as Terra did, if not even just a teensy bit better (Terra hoped so, being the generous sort).

She sped up her fucking, bit by bit, and soon she was pounding into Athene's cunt, and now it felt so good she only barely managed to notice that her own body was beginning to glow, too, just like the dildo—only brighter, it seemed, the glow lighting up more and more of Athene's bedroom. As it grew brighter, it also began to spread to Athene's body, coating her with its ethereal light, and soon they were lighting up the entire room, flickers of light dancing across its every surface in the most marvelous, magical way.

A sudden bright flash shocked Terra's eyes, and she squeezed them shut to block it out. Just as she shut her eyes, she and Athene orgasmed, only a second or two apart. This time Terra magically created the bubble to contain their sounds, not even noticing that she was doing it, because she was coming so incredibly hard she was aware of very little other than her orgasm and the gorgeous body beneath her that was causing it.

The glow disappeared the second she stopped coming. "Athene…Athene…what just happened?" she said between gasps for breath.

"I have no idea whatsoever," Athene said, collapsing to the bed. "But whatever it was, it was pretty damn cool."

They lay down next to each other, their faces flushed. Terra had to know, though, if that had been her doing. Had it? "Was that me? I mean, did I do those things?"

"It wasn't *me*, sweetie. I didn't…I didn't know you could do that stuff. All that magic—the glow, the bubble…" Athene looked a little shocked as she said this. Had Terra worried her? Had she done something wrong? "You seem to have a bit more power than you used to. That's awesome! High five?"

Terra laughed at that. "So that's good, what I just did?"

"That's *great*, actually. Congratulations, honey!" Athene kissed Terra on the lips. The kiss turned into a second one, and soon they were making out again.

"Wanna go again?" she asked Athene between kisses.

"Maybe in a day or two" was the answer.

"Let's make it tomorrow afternoon. I don't think I can wait even a whole day to see you again. Not if having sex with you has gotten even more amazing."

"I guess I'm up for that. No, I'm *totally* up for that."

Terra realized then how thirsty she was, and so she began to struggle her way off the bed to get some water from the bathroom. But moments after she was fully upright, her hand jumped up into the air, and a tall glass of opalescent liquid appeared in her hand. She shrieked, and then the door to Athene's bedroom began to swing wide open.

"Shit!" Athene reached for Terra, but Terra was faster. She dashed into Athene's bathroom and hid behind its halfway-open door.

"What is it?" It was one of the guard's voices, she realized—Bacab.

"Oh, Bacab," she heard Athene say in a calm voice, "It was nothing. I just thought I saw a mouse."

"Shall I search for it and kill it for you?"

"Kill it? No, no, I like mice. It just surprised me, that's all, ran over my foot as I was getting into bed."

Terra's next thought was that Athene had been naked when the door began to open. Hopefully Bacab wasn't getting a free show. Ha—that was the *last* of her worries. What if Bacab caught her in there? What would...but before she could come up with any more worries, she heard him tell Athene good night and walk out of the room.

After Terra heard the door click shut, Athene walked over to the bathroom and eased open the door. Thank Goddess, Terra thought, as she saw that Athene was covered up, wearing a knee-length cotton nightgown.

"You'd better leave through this door instead," Athene said, and kissed Terra on the cheek, hugging her close. She pressed Terra's underwear into her hands, along with a doorway stone. "I'll see you soon, okay? How about tomorrow at four?"

Terra shimmied back into her panties and bra. "Sounds great. I'll be here, promise." Athene shut the bathroom door, and Terra waited a moment, then put down the doorway stone and opened the door, walking through it and back into her bedroom. She lay down on the room's bed, feeling somewhat exhausted.

Onyx walked over to her, rubbing himself up against her calves. "Where'd that glass come from?" he asked her. It was only then that she realized she was still holding the mysterious glass, full of equally mysterious liquid.

"No idea, none at all," she told him. "It just...appeared in my hand when I was in Athene's room, out of nowhere. I thought about how thirsty I was, and then—boom!—there it was."

"Are you still thirsty?"

"I guess I am. Are you suggesting I drink a strange glass of glowing liquid that appeared out of nowhere?" She peered down at the glass, then moved it nearer to her face, giving the liquid a closer look. It was moving slightly, or at least it was beneath the surface, swirls of glowing rainbows dancing around inside the glass.

"I am suggesting that, in fact." Onyx sounded entirely certain when he said this. "It looks like something you should drink, based on what the glass contains."

"Oh?" she said softly. "And what's that?"

"It's supposed to bring you a vision. Of the Other Side."

"The Other...do you mean what I think you mean?"

"I do. Maybe it's from your...well, there's only one way to find out."

Terra knew what word would have come after "your" in his sentence. And perhaps it was from her. She brought the glass to her lips and took a small sip. It tasted sweet, like honey. "Huh, I wouldn't have guessed it would be so delicious," she murmured as the taste spread across her tongue.

Something was now shimmering in front of the bed, and a figure began to appear before her, pale and almost invisible. But the figure's face was clear enough. Onyx had been right, she realized with a soft smile. It was *her*—it was her mother.

"Terra, my darling, darling daughter. You're just as beautiful as I thought you would be. And just as powerful, too.

I can feel it coming from you, even though we are so far apart." Her mother's ghostly hand reached out and cupped Terra's face, where a tear was slowly running down her cheek.

"H-hi, Mom. It's so…it's really good to see you."

"It's wonderful to see you as well, Terra. I have things to tell you, but I haven't much time."

"What? What do you need to tell me?"

"You will have help along the way, as you travel the roads and the lands and continue on your quest. I have made sure of that. But you must watch out for the man with flaming horns, as he may send you over to the Other Side. He won't stop at anything to gain the power of the Werths. Not that he needs it."

"The man with horns? Who is he?"

But instead of answering her, her mother Nerit began to fade. "I love you. I hope we will meet again, perhaps soon. I love you, Ter—"

And then her mother disappeared, as did the glass. "Mom, come back! Please!" But Nerit was gone.

Onyx jumped into her lap, nuzzling against her and purring. "She'll be back, Terra, I just know it."

"I hope you're right. I hope to Goddess you're right."

Still in only her underwear, she got into bed. The sheets were deliciously soft against her bare skin, and she fell asleep in just a few minutes. She spent the night dreaming of Athene, chasing her through fields and forests, but never quite catching up to her, never managing to grab her and pull her into her arms.

CHAPTER TEN

In the morning, Terra's first thought was of her mother's visit. It was not a good thought to start a day with, so instead she rolled onto her side and gave Onyx a good, long belly scratch. "What do you say you and I go scare up some breakfast?"

"Mmm, how about some catfish?"

"I'm thinking more along the lines of some eggs and toast, but I'll see what I can do for you." She got up out of bed and put on her change of clothes. If only she'd brought more than one, because it was a little embarrassing to wear the same thing two days in a row. Just as she was thinking that, her blouse began to feel a little tighter. She looked down, and now she was wearing a black-and-red houndstooth vest over a white T-shirt.

"You've really got to get your magic in check, young lady," Onyx said as walked over to the door. "We can't have you pulling any rabbits out of hats among the humans."

"Yeah, I know. But it seems I don't have much control over it at this point. It's all new to me, you know. And I didn't even tell you about what happened last night."

Onyx turned back toward her, and it almost seemed like he had an expression of mild disgust in his eyes. "I can only hope you never will, based on the look on your face."

"It was…I glowed and made the magic bubble and…it was amazing. And very surprising."

"I bet it was, Terra, but we need to get going. We still have a lot of quest to accomplish in the next few days, you know."

"I do know, little kitty." Terra made sure everything was in her travel bag and glanced around the lovely hotel room one last time. Then she picked up her bag and the room key and went to the door, opening it and stepping into the hallway. It wasn't where the door had taken her the previous night, she thought, a realization that came with a touch of sadness.

After checking out, she went to her car with Onyx and drove back to The Town Restaurant, which was bustling and full of people enjoying hearty breakfasts. It was very likely they were all about to go to work. She wasn't, though, because for once she didn't have to gobble down a quick bite and rush off to start scrubbing whatever she was ordered to scrub. She might have been taking her life into her hands, going on this quest, but being able to sit down and take her time with breakfast was a luxury she had rarely enjoyed before this morning. She ordered the special, a lox-and-chive omelet, and asked for extra lox in a to-go box.

Her crush, the redheaded waitress, was working this morning, but she wasn't the one waiting on Terra, so she only got the occasional glimpse of the cute, slightly older woman. Today her hair was in a ponytail, her red curls bouncing a little as she hurried back and forth across the room. At one point, she noticed Terra looking at her, but before Terra could glance away, the waitress grinned at her and winked. Was that woman *flirting* with her?

Yes, she was, Terra realized, as soon, the woman walked straight over to where she was sitting and eating her omelet. The waitress placed her hand on her right hip and grinned down at Terra. "I get off in about an hour. You free then?"

"I'm...not, actually. I was just about to leave town. And I'm also kind of taken."

"A lovely young butch like you? Of course you are. Well, if you change your mind, either about leaving town or being taken, just tell me, will you, hon?" She walked off, and Terra found herself wondering if the waitress was swinging her hips in that extremely sensual way just for her.

But just for her or not, Terra was still leaving town, and she was decidedly taken. She paid her bill and left, glancing back at the waitress one last time. She was hot, for sure, but she hadn't even come close to tempting Terra away from the quest—or, more important, tempting her away from Athene.

On the way back to her car, she heard someone calling her name. Looking around, she saw Jeremy dashing across the street. "Wait, Terra! I need to talk to you!" He was panting a little as he reached her, which made it seem like he was a bit out of shape. Either that or he'd been running for a while.

"What is it, Jeremy? I'm just about to leave."

"I know, I know. Just, first, I wanted to tell you something."

"Yes?"

"Stop by the gem shop about an hour away from Missiou. The women who run the place, they'll want to help you out. Tell them...who was it...Nerit. Tell them Nerit sent you." Terra gasped as he said this, but Jeremy didn't seem to notice, continuing after a few panting breaths. "That's what my brother told me to say to you, before he said good-bye." Jeremy looked close to tears as he said this, and so Terra placed her hand on his shoulder.

"I'm sorry to hear he's gone, Jeremy."

"Well, we never got along, anyway. It's fine. He's in a better place, yadda yadda yadda." Jeremy started to walk away then, but before he crossed the street, he turned back to Terra, shielding his eyes against the sun. "You're obviously a good person, young lady. I hope you succeed in your travels. Good luck and all of that."

She watched him walk off and felt a little—or maybe a lot—touched by what he had said. But it was time to leave, so she got into her car next to Onyx and set down the box of salmon. "You get any of that on this car's interior—"

"And I become a very tiny fur rug. Got it."

Terra found she was a little sad to see the last of the town reflected in her rearview mirror, but not because of the hot waitress. No, it was because of Jeremy, and Katherine, too, and maybe…maybe a few other things. But she steadied her emotions, because she still had a lot of road to cover, of course, a lot of road and three more parts to the quest. Hopefully they would be as easy to accomplish as the first part, but she doubted it. The first part had been almost too easy, although a noticeable amount of sadness had come along with what she'd done.

She turned on the car's radio as Missiou disappeared into the distance, watching the road ahead of her and humming along with Johnny Cash. Onyx had finished his salmon by then, and she learned that although he knew all the words to "A Boy Named Sue," he really didn't know the notes.

"God, Onyx, you couldn't carry a tune in a stainless-steel bucket."

"I happen to think I have a very nice singing voice, little lady." And then he was back to torturing one of her favorite songs, somewhat like how she'd seen him torture a mouse once. Only this was a hell of a lot more painful to experience.

The radio seemed to play all her favorite songs, she realized after a few miles. Probably something Athene had thrown into the magic she'd used on the car. What a sweetheart. She was getting a little distracted thinking about Athene, thoughts that started out entirely benign and then began to take a turn for the wicked. Athene in their last encounter, fucking her strap-on... Athene sucking on it...Athene taking it up the...

"Hey, idiot, watch the road!" Onyx yelled, and Terra realized she was starting to drive right off it, straight toward a large tree. She quickly corrected the car, and then she thought she saw something in her rearview mirror. Were those flames back behind...She shook her head a little, and just like that, the image was gone. It had been a mirage, she decided. After all, it was an uncomfortably hot day.

"Sorry, man," she told him. "I kind of got distracted."

"I could tell from that evil grin on your face. But I don't have any plans to become a snack for carrion, so keep your thoughts on the road and off Athene."

She almost told him about what she might have seen behind them, but then she reconsidered. No reason to bring up a hallucination to Onyx. He'd probably just make fun of her, the little brat.

Her attention back on the road like Onyx had requested (ordered?), she noticed that just ahead of them, on the right, was a driveway, with a sign over it that said, RISING MOON & SETTING SUN—GEMSTONES AND WONDERS.

"That must be the place Jeremy was talking about." Terra slowed down and turned onto the dirt driveway.

"You're just going to take that strange man's advice?"

"He's the reason I completed the first part of the quest, Onyx. And he said something about my mom sending me here."

"And you're going to trust him?" Onyx sounded incredulous at the thought, but then he shook his head and sighed. "I suppose we could both use a few wonders in our lives. Go ahead."

"I already have," she said under her breath. They'd just reached a large, two-story house, painted every color of the rainbow. Normally, a house like that would have looked tacky to Terra, but whoever had painted this one had somehow made it into one of the most beautiful things she'd ever seen. She realized as she got out of the car, Onyx not far behind her, that it sparkled in the sunlight, and when she reached the door, she saw that beautiful stones were placed in random—but somehow perfect—places all across the front of the building. The front window next to the door had an OPEN sign placed in it, so she opened the screen door and walked inside.

Once she was in the building, it took her eyes a few moments to adjust, but Onyx was already glancing around. "These rocks are just beautiful," he said.

"Glad to hear it, kitty cat," said a voice.

Terra inhaled sharply. "You can hear him?"

A woman, probably about thirty years old, and with waist-length, gold-colored hair, was walking into the room. "Sure can. I'm Sun, by the way," she said, gently shaking Terra's hand, her palm and fingers surprisingly warm as they touched Terra's skin. The room almost seemed brighter with Sun in it, and Terra liked her, despite the fact they'd only just met.

"And I'm Moon." Another woman walked into the room, and while Sun was a fair bit more than mildly beautiful, this woman practically glowed with beauty. Or perhaps she *was* glowing. Her short, silver hair seemed to put off light, more and more as she approached Sun and Terra.

"You must be the people who run this place. Your house, or store, or whatever—it's beautiful." Just like you, she thought, glancing from woman to woman.

"Thank you," Sun said, placing her hand on Terra's shoulder and beginning to guide her toward some stairs.

"Yes, thank you. For both compliments."

Terra's mouth fell open at Moon's words, and the two women laughed together. "Yes," Sun said, "we can hear talking cats *and* read minds. Aren't we terrifying?" But Terra wasn't scared at all, not hesitating for even a second before she followed Sun up the narrow staircase.

She heard Moon climbing the stairs behind them, and then Onyx rushed by all three of them. He curled up in a spot of sun at the top of the stairs, sun that was coming in from a large, round window in the roof.

The second floor held a bed, a table with three chairs, and a small kitchen area, complete with fridge, sink, and oven. Everything in there was either painted gold or silver. Or maybe everything is made *out* of gold and silver, Terra thought.

"Would you care for some tea, my dear?" Sun asked.

"I think that would be nice." She turned to Sun and smiled at her.

"I hope green tea will be all right with you. We have a pitcher of it sitting in the fridge, perfect for a hot day like this, although I do get quite a bit thirstier on hot days than my sweetheart does." Moon kissed Sun on the cheek and walked over to the fridge, removing a tall pitcher of pale-green liquid and a plate of lemon slices. She placed those on the table and got three square glasses out of a cupboard above the stove, placing one in front of each chair. Terra noticed that both women moved with a smooth, flowing grace. She had also noticed that these two women appeared to be a couple. They seemed to be very much in love, and seeing them being affectionate with each other made her rather happy. Just like her and Athene, although these two seemed like they'd been together a fair bit longer.

Terra sat down at the table, and the two women joined her. Sun poured tea into each of the glasses, and Terra picked hers up once it was full, taking a long swallow of what turned out to be very delicious tea.

"So, who sent you here?" Sun asked, leaning forward.

"Yes, who? After all, we are only visible to a very small selection of beings, so whoever it was must be pretty important."

She felt a little uncomfortable with the woman staring at her so intently. "Can't you just...read my mind about that?"

"We could, but, as Moon reminded me as we came up here, I was forgetting my manners when I did that," Sun said with a smile. "I do find it helps keep me a few steps ahead of our guests, but she—actually, we...we thought there was something special about you."

"Yes, you remind us of someone else. A woman who, not so long ago, also came to us." Moon placed her hand over Sun's and gave it a squeeze. "She was in love with a human, you see, and she wanted to know if there was any way to fall out of love with him. That or change him into a Magic One."

"You aren't talking about..." Terra looked down at the table for a long moment, then looked up and back at the two women. "You aren't talking about my mom, are you?"

"Of course!" Moon slapped the table, causing Terra to jump a little at the sudden movement and sound. "You must be her daughter—Nerit's daughter. How is she?"

"She's...not around anymore. At least, not until last night." Terra sighed. "Now it's like she's everywhere, back from the dead, almost. Only, not really. Not really at *all*." Now she felt like slapping the table. Or slapping whoever was screwing with her like this, sending her visions of her dead mother, visions and messages. Maybe they would prove to be helpful, but did the help she might be receiving have to hurt so fucking much?

"You look so sad, Nerit's daughter." Moon placed a cool hand over Terra's right hand, and Sun placed a warm hand over her left. Each woman's touch made her feel somewhat more centered and stable, and made a bit of the pain she was feeling begin to drift away, too.

"Are you using magic on me?"

"Just a touch," Moon told her. "Just a touch."

"But you seem to have some of your own magic, young lady." Sun grinned at her.

"Some and then some more," Moon said, and with those words the women removed their hands, soon holding each other's instead.

Terra downed the last of her tea, trying to fight off the sadness that seemed bound to return at any moment. But it didn't, not for the next few minutes, at least, minutes she spent drinking another glass of tea and listening to the two women speak.

"Your mother had great power, and it seems like some of it is finally flowing down into you." Sun lifted her glass off the table, and it floated up out of her hand and began to lazily spin back and forth a few inches above her open hand. "It seems like on this journey you are on, which we're guessing is not all that different than your mother's…it seems like you will need it, too."

"Yes, because we see a threat heading toward you, a threat that may not be far off." The glass began to spin faster, and faster, becoming a blur as it spun, until it dropped to the table with a loud *thump*, tea sloshing over its sides and running toward Terra's hands. She yanked them back and threw them up, and the tea stopped halfway across the table, flowing back to the glass and back over its sides until the table was dry and all the tea was back where it had been.

"I didn't…did one of you do that?" She glanced from woman to woman, but they both looked genuinely surprised.

Sun spoke first. "We certainly didn't make the glass do that—"

"And we certainly didn't clean up the mess it caused, either. I think the second part was all you, daughter of Nerit, but that first part—" Both women shivered a little as Moon said those last four words. "You listen, and you listen carefully. Watch out for the man with horns."

"Yeah, I know—the man with flaming horns, who will kill me if I give him the chance. My mom told me that, too." She tried to sound bold as she said this, and she decided she'd succeeded, although she didn't get the desired response.

A worried glance passed from Moon to Sun. "Don't you take this advice lightly, young lady," Sun said, her voice sharp and hard. "If you've heard it before, it must be important. Especially if your mother came all the way from the Other Side to tell you about him."

"But now it's time for you to get going." Moon rose from the table, and so Terra got up too. "You obviously have more important things to do than chat with two old women."

"Old? But you look so—never mind." Terra had just remembered that age was sometimes *really* just a number with the magically inclined, at least if they happened to be powerful, and these two sure seemed like they were. "I'll be off now, then. Come on, Onyx, let's go back to the car."

"But…sun! Warm!"

She nudged his butt with her foot, and he hissed halfheartedly at her, then got up and went down the stairs. Extra slowly, of course.

Terra was halfway out the door when she felt a cool hand on her arm. Moon's. She turned around all the way and saw that the woman was holding what looked to be a column-shaped roll of pale-gray cloth. "What is it, Moon?"

"I saw something, right when you reached the bottom of the stairs. You'll need this, at the end of your journey." Moon held the cloth out to Terra. Her face looked paler than it had before, and Terra almost thought she looked a little scared. "Take it, please. It will both help with defense and help with… finding something, I'm not sure what. The vision got kind of hazy at that part."

"Thanks, Moon. But what is it?" Terra took the roll of cloth. It felt somewhat heavy in her hand, clearly not just a bolt of fabric.

"It's a spyglass. A very special one. If you use it you can find things that do not wish to be found."

"What kinds of things, Moon?"

"Good, bad, I don't know. Not yet. But take care, young lady, take care. And...yes, you will need some protection along the way, so if a raccoon happens to offer it, and he is joined by a stag, accept their help."

"A...raccoon? How could a raccoon help me?" Terra was a little bit confused at Moon's advice. Along with that little bit of confusion was also a little bit of fear, fear that was causing a small, hard knot to form in her stomach.

"You should go now, before he catches up to you." And without another word, Moon pushed Terra out the door and slammed it shut behind her.

"How fucking rude can you get!" She turned back toward the door and glared at it, but deep down she knew Moon meant the best. Still, she had to stop in just a few hours, because she and Athene had an arranged meeting that afternoon, and nothing could talk her out of making that stop. Not even Moon's vision could do that. After all, she barely knew the woman, so how was she supposed to know whether she should trust her advice?

Clouds had started to fill the sky while she had been in the house, and as she got into the car, little drops of rain began to hit the windows of the Jag.

"Looks like we're in for a storm," she said to Onyx.

"Looks like."

Hopefully, Terra thought, as she drove along beneath the dark storm clouds and through the rain, this was the *only* storm they were in for.

CHAPTER ELEVEN

A few hours and a fair number of miles later, it was time for Terra to visit Athene. She pulled into a decrepit-looking parking lot in front of a warehouse that looked long forgotten, with peeling paint and broken windows. "Doesn't seem like a good place to pull over, Terra." Onyx placed his paws up on the window, slowly moving his head back and forth. "Looks bad, girl, it looks very bad. I wouldn't go in there for all the mice and hot male cats in the world. Nope."

"You're lucky. You don't have to. Just wait in the locked car. I'll be back before you know it."

"Bitch." He said this quietly, but she thought he most likely intended for her to hear it.

"I'll stop somewhere nice for a late lunch after this, I promise."

"Somewhere *very* nice."

"And here, this should keep you busy, at least for a while." Terra reached into the lunch sack she'd left in the backseat and got out the last can of cat food, peeling off the lid and placing it on the floor in front of his seat.

Onyx climbed down to the food and started eating. "I still want that fancy lunch, too," he mumbled between bites.

"Sure, kitty, sure. Now, let's see if this works with car doors, too." She took the doorway stone out of her travel bag and placed it next to the car door. Then she opened it and saw that the stone had indeed worked, because there was Athene, sitting on her bed and reading a book. An erotic book, from the looks of the cover.

"Couldn't wait for me? You had to get started early?"

Athene jumped. "You scared me!" She got up and placed a hand on her hip, the other one still gripping her book.

"You haven't changed a bit. Didn't even drop your book, did you?"

"I wasn't *that* scared. Not scared enough to risk damaging a brand-new book."

They both laughed at that, and Terra shook her head a little as she did. Then she lifted her hand, placing her fingers against Athene's chin, tilting it up to look right into her eyes. She stared down at Athene with an expression she hoped showed that her interest was not really on the book, but on Athene. Then she asked, "Now, what might you be reading? I thought I saw two women on the cover, one lying over the other's lap, and I think there might have been some lingerie and rope in the artwork as well." She reached for the book, but Athene pulled it away, taking a bookmark out of the back of it and marking her spot. She then went over to the window, placing the book on the windowsill, and slowly, and very sensually, walked back toward Terra. "Just doing some research," she said with a sly grin. "That's all."

"What, precisely, were you 'researching'?" She made air quotes when she said that last word, a slightly sardonic smile spreading across her face to match her sarcasm.

"Oh, this and that. Bondage, domination. The usual. And why do you think I might be doing that, researching such dirty, dirty things?" Athene continued to walk toward her, her hips making subtle thrusts and her words carrying not-so-subtle implications, all of it telling Terra everything she needed to know.

"What might you have in mind, then? Since it seems as if you're the one in charge?"

"It's not 'as if,' it's how it *is*, my pet." Athene was right in front of her now, and she cupped Terra's chin, pulling her head down until they were staring directly into each other's eyes once again.

Terra felt a little nervous at this new turn of events, but her body didn't seem entirely nervous, as her cunt was getting rather wet just from Athene's grip and the hard look in her eyes. "What are you going to do to me, then?" she asked, her voice more steady than she currently felt.

"Oh, whatever I want, of course." Athene's face held a feline, womanly smile, one that spoke of all the things women were good for, at least in the bedroom. "Now take off your clothes," she told Terra, "and get on the bed."

"Sure thing." Terra didn't like how her voice had shook a little as she said this, and her body was shaky, too, her legs not really in agreement with the idea of taking off her pants, and her hands performing at slightly less than their normal degree of usefulness, as well. But goddamn it, had she ever been even close to this wet before?

She climbed onto the bed and half-sat, half-kneeled, her feet off to one side. Now she was completely naked, and Athene was still fully dressed. Terra felt as if she were even more than naked because of this, and she was worried that her body was betraying her every thought. What would Athene do with this knowledge, this realization of how easy it was to take over her will? And her flesh?

Athene climbed onto the bed and ran the back of her hand down Terra's side, over her hip, and then, in a lightning-fast movement, she shoved her palm against Terra's cunt, causing her to jump and gasp at the sudden pressure against her crotch. She knew Athene would notice how wet she was, because, in fact, she was so aroused by now that it almost seemed like the wetness would start gushing out any moment, gushing out and flowing down Athene's arm. "Fuck, you're wet, you're so *wet*." Athene grinned then, a grin coupled with the most sadistic look Terra had ever seen cross her mild-mannered face.

"Get on your knees, while I put on the strap-on. Are you all right with being tied up and having your ass fucked? Because you damn well better be."

"Yes, yes, I am," she answered, surprising herself with her rapid consent. But Athene didn't look surprised at all, merely pleased, which made Terra even more surprised at herself. How could Athene have expected this of her? But she wasn't even slightly shocked at how easy it had been to talk Terra into doing two things she'd never, ever done before—two things that she'd agreed to, just like that!

So she got onto her hands and knees, and she watched as Athene uncoiled some beautiful, dark-blue rope. It turned out to be two lengths, and Athene placed each length on opposite sides of the bed's top. With a wave of her hand, each blue rope began to wrap around Terra's wrists, and they pulled her forward a little and tied themselves to the bed's posts. Meanwhile, Athene occupied herself by running her nails up and down Terra's back, starting softly and then getting a little rougher as the nails traveled down her sloping skin. It never hurt too much, staying just barely on the right side of too painful, and Terra sighed and shivered at the pressure, at each slow raking of Athene's nails down her naked, restrained body.

"Good, very good. I'm going to get out the strap-on now."

Terra couldn't see anything Athene was doing. She could only hear quiet rustling sounds, what must have been Athene pulling it over her legs and hips and then letting it magically adjust itself. Then she felt Athene get onto the bed behind her, and the dildo began to press against her asshole. It seemed...

bigger than she remembered it being. And how well would it go in without lube? "Is it bigger than the last one?" she asked, hoping her voice wasn't shaking as much as she thought it seemed to be. Her heart had sped up a little too, and she worried her body's tension would make it hurt. She'd never had more than two fingers back there, and now this? Now a rather thick-feeling dildo was going to slide into her tightest hole?

"It most definitely is bigger," came Athene's voice. "A fair amount bigger. But don't worry. It'll go in just fine, my little anal virgin." And "go in just fine" it did, as with one quick, hard thrust it went straight in. All...the...way...in, Terra thought as she gasped at its sudden intrusion. But, thankfully, it didn't hurt. Not even a little bit. No, instead, it felt rather good. More than good. A lot more than good! And it only got better as, at a far slower speed, Athene pulled back her hips and it slid out, farther and farther, until it was out almost all the way, until only the tip remained in. Terra couldn't believe how good it felt, and she said just that. "Wow, Athene, just...how could it possibly feel so good? I mean...I mean, no offense, but your fingers never felt like this." And then she said something far less intelligent, just a string of expletives and moans, as Athene wiggled her hips a little, causing the dildo to wiggle, too.

"It feels good to me, too," Athene said, "but if you don't mind, less talking and more fucking." She began to fuck Terra, then, sliding the tip of the dildo a little deeper in and then all the way out, stretching her wide open all over again each time she shoved the thick tip of the dildo back inside her. "Remember, I can feel it, too, and you feel so...fuck...deliciously tight, gripping me like a strong little fist. I'm so glad I came up with this idea. So...fucking...glad."

With each of those three words, Athene thrust into her, then out, and Terra sighed and gasped and moaned with each delicious bit of pressure. It felt even better than when Athene had used the magic strap-on on her cunt. Apparently her lovely, lovely girlfriend had made a few very nice adjustments to the dildo's magic, because every thrust felt like a miniature orgasm, starting all around where the dildo pressed against her and flowing across every centimeter of the surrounding skin. And yes, she realized with a grin, as she strained against her restraints, each movement of her skin against the rope felt orgasmic, too.

"You're the best, Athene," she told her, as Athene continued to fuck her with what she decided was immense competence.

"Glad to hear it, Terra. Now shut up and just concentrate on how much you like having your ass fucked. Because it's only going to get better...you're only going to like it more with each second I spend inside you."

And goddamn, if she hadn't hit the nail squarely on the head. Each time the dildo inched in and out, the miniature orgasms grew, until it felt like she was coming through every pore of her nude, sweaty skin. She barely even noticed Athene envelop them in the bubble, it felt so damn good; she barely even noticed how loud they each became with each thrust of the dildo, with every undulation of Athene's hips. She barely even noticed it when she began to pull at her restraints, just so she could drive the dildo in deeper, and deeper still, until they both cried out in unison, so very loud.

When their twin orgasms had reached their end, they collapsed onto the bed in a sweaty, limp heap. "That was...that was...it was, well, *you* know...right?" Terra figured Athene would understand what she meant.

"Yeah, it was...totally...it was...wow."

"Maybe we'll learn how to talk again soon?"

Athene laughed when she said this and replied, in between pants for breath, "Sure, we can learn...how to move again, too...after we've...remembered how to talk."

"Too much pleasure, can't think." Terra slowly felt her strength returning, much slower than usual. "Forgot to do a spell to help us out this time?"

"Nope, but apparently I underestimated how strong it needed to be. By a whole, big lot of an amount."

"You just don't want me to leave." She had intended it as a joke, but Athene's sad sigh seemed to say it didn't strike her as all that funny.

"Maybe I don't."

The ropes disappeared, and Terra rolled over, staring up at Athene and seeing how sad she looked. "It's not like we've been apart that long between each time we've met in here. No longer than usual, actually."

"I know, but it's not that at all. It's...it's that I don't even really know where you are, or if you're safe, or if you're even still—"

"Oh, honey!" She pulled Athene to her, hugging her fast and hard. "I'm fine, totally safe," she said quietly into Athene's ear. "I doubt there'll be anything dangerous at all on this quest."

"I don't know, but...I hope not. I really, really hope not."

But now it was time for her to go, so after putting on her clothes, she hugged Athene one last time. Not *the* last time, though. In fact, she would be back that very night, and as she opened the door and got back into her car, she found she was already looking forward to it.

Then she heard a knock on her car's window and saw someone staring right at her, and she screamed as loud as she could.

Chapter Twelve

D amn, woman, can you ever scream!" It was then Terra realized that the face and the knocking fist belonged to Pan.

"Fuck." She took a deep breath and moved the doorway stone back into her bag. Then she got out of the car and stood next to the young man who happened to be part of her competition.

"You're...did you steal that car? I may be wrong, but I'm pretty sure a man was driving it last. His name was—"

"Saturn. Yeah, I know."

"How, exactly, did you know that?" He tapped his foot on the ground, a foot that was wearing a sky-blue cowboy boot, and Terra couldn't help wanting a pair of her own. A pair of them and her man-disguise back. But it was too late for that. She'd been found out, and she only hoped she had been right about both Pan's orientation and his trustworthiness.

"Here's the truth. My name's Terra, I'm really a maid at the Werths', and Athene and I are in love. Very much in love."

"I suppose you know my secret too, then."

Onyx had gotten out of the car and was now rubbing back and forth across Pan's ankles. "Yes," he purred, "I can tell a fellow lover of men from ten paces."

Pan won himself some points then by bending down and scratching the cat's head. "Is this seemingly gay, talking cat your familiar?"

"Nope, he's Athene's. I don't have very much magic...or at least I didn't when I started on the quest. That seems to be changing, though. Quickly." She shut the car door and leaned up against it. Pan joined her there a few moments later.

"Just so you know, you don't have to worry about me trying to steal her from you. After all, if Onyx were a man—a very cute man—I'd prefer him to you. I might as well be honest."

"Yeah, but he's a cat, and I'm a lesbian, and this whole fucking thing is just a huge mess. Or, at least, a really, really huge challenge."

"You seem like you might be up for it, though. Actually, I could feel you through the car door, Terra. You feel much stronger than you did at the dinner, too. I'm pretty sure...yeah, you might actually be a bit past me. And while I'm no all-powerful being, I'm not exactly pathetic, either." He was looking at her now, and she could feel his stare passing through her outer body and into the place where she felt her magic must lie.

Pan reached out to her then, moving his hand toward the middle of her chest, and then he leapt back. Or was he thrown back? Terra couldn't tell, but his sudden movement made her tense all the same.

"You *are* more powerful than me. The way you pushed me back, that pulse of magic—I felt so...so much. You might have a chance after all. No—you definitely have a chance."

"Thanks, Pan. That means a lot to me. Are you going to keep pursuing the quest, though?" She couldn't help asking him, even though she figured it didn't matter either way.

"I am—I have to. But I'll try really hard to lose. Not that losing will be very challenging, at least now that you seem to be ahead of me on the magical-power spectrum. Way ahead."

"Great!" Terra felt a surge of energy at his compliment, although maybe that surge hadn't come from his compliment. Maybe it had come from her newfound powers instead? Wherever it had come from, it was more than welcome, because she still had three more challenges of the quest to get to and to get through.

"Which way are you headed?" Terra had noticed that up ahead of them the road forked, and she guessed it was likely they would go the same way.

"I'm going left. Or right. Why don't you tell me which way you're going, actually, and then I'll decide?"

Terra laughed and was grinning at him when she said, "Are you saying what I think you're saying?"

"I may be."

"I'm going...let's see..." She paused for a second and closed her eyes. A strong pull was coming from the right, she realized, a strong pull and—was it raining? Her clothes felt wet, suddenly, so she opened her eyes and looked up, but no, the sky had cleared while she'd been in the car, not a cloud in sight. "I'm going right. And this may sound like a weird question, but do your clothes feel wet to you?"

"Not any more than they usually do on a hot day like this. A little damp under the armpits, but other than that, no. Why do you ask?"

"I just thought I felt...never mind. So, which way are you going then?"

"Opposite of you, of course."

"Thanks. Really, thanks."

"Hey, it's the least I can do for someone who seems to be in love. I've never been so lucky myself, but someday, perhaps."

"I haven't either," Onyx piped up, nuzzling against Pan's boots. "Okay, Terra, let's get going."

"The cat's right," Terra said. "We should all get going." Especially me, she thought.

"Yep. Good luck, then, to both of you. May the best woman win."

Terra chuckled. She watched him walk back to his vehicle—a black, two-seater sports car—and waited for him to drive off. He honked his horn twice and then started his car, pulling back onto the highway and doing just as he'd said he would, driving up to the fork and turning to the left. *What a sweet man.* Maybe someday he'd be as lucky as she was and find someone as awesome and terrific as Athene. Only a whole lot more male.

She got back into the car after she nudged Onyx inside. "You liked him, didn't you?" she asked the still-purring cat.

"Maybe I did. What do you care?"

"Oh, nothing." She glanced at Onyx out of the corner of her eyes. He sighed and curled up in his seat, and so she started the car, driving the few hundred feet up to the fork in the road. She turned right, because that was the direction she felt she had to go. How did she know that, though? She wondered about it for a bit, but it didn't really matter, she realized, because she was positive she was going toward wherever the next part of the quest was located. Her clothes still felt strangely damp, and she shivered a little despite the warmth on her bare skin. Hopefully this was just a clue—that she was close to the water she was supposed to drink. A clue, and not a bad sign instead.

It seemed that she *had* chosen the right direction (or perhaps her body had chosen it, who knew?) because soon she came to a small bridge about fifty feet above a midsized river. "I'll be back soon, Onyx," she said, getting out of the car. "See you then, okay?"

"Be careful." Onyx sounded a little nervous, but she figured he just wasn't looking forward to being left alone again. Silly cat.

"I will be," Terra told him.

She shut the door and walked the rest of the way across the bridge, then began inching her way down the steep path that led to the water. It was beautiful there, with rays of sunlight sparkling on the flowing water in a most lovely way. Once she reached the bank of the river, she stood still for a moment, just taking in the beauty of nature all around her, as well as the water rushing past her feet. Was this the water she was supposed to drink, though? Something like energy was coming off it, but it didn't feel especially strong.

Then she yelped. Something had grabbed her ankle, something that looked like a hand made out of water. It was only seconds before she was yanked into the water and was being pulled down, deep down beneath its surface, much deeper down than should have been possible. But there was no time for her to think about what was possible and what wasn't, because she couldn't breathe, and the water's surface was moving farther and farther away. It was getting dark…everything was getting dark…

A thought of Athene flashed through her head then, and she noticed she was starting to glow. It was bright again now, and a woman's voice said, "Bring her to us."

She could breathe again. She could breathe again and she was on dry land, hard, sharp rocks digging into her hands and knees. Terra sucked in breath after breath, her chest heaving, and then, all her strength was now gone, and she collapsed onto the ground in a soggy, limp heap. "Am I…safe now?" She forced the words out between gasps of breath.

Three shadows came closer and closer to her soaking-wet, completely exhausted self. She sincerely hoped they wouldn't be a threat to her, because she felt incredibly weak, and magic or not, she wouldn't be able to fight anyone off.

The three shadows drew nearer, shrinking bit by bit, until she saw three pairs of sandaled feet. Not merely sandaled feet, though—*perfect*, absolutely *perfect* sandaled feet. She'd never want to change a single thing about those feet. And as her eyes traveled up—up long, elegant legs, awe-inspiring curves, and long, swan-like necks, they finally rested on the three most beautiful, most perfect faces she had ever seen, each face a different shade of blue, but all utterly equal in their splendor. "Are you...goddesses?" she asked, her voice annoyingly full of awe.

The three women (whom she now realized were all naked) laughed at her words, their laughter like beautiful birdsong or the wind whispering against velvet, velvet or, perhaps, silk.

"Goddesses?" said the one on the left.

"You think we're goddesses?" asked the one who stood in the middle.

"No." The third laughed. "We are just three women with dirty clothes. You see how we are all nude, do you not?"

"Kind of...hard to miss, with bodies like yours. Fuck, excuse me." Terra slowly pushed herself up from the ground, politely refusing the women's hands when they held them out. "No, I'm worried that if I touch you, any of you, I'll never want to leave."

"What—" said the one on the left.

"A smart—" said the one in the middle.

"Girl," said the one on the right. "But there's still the problem of our dirty clothes." She gestured toward a bucket, overflowing with clothing. "Can you get them clean? No one has been able to, so far."

"If you can," said the one in the middle, "we will let you drink our water and gain its power."

"You will? But...why can't you get the clothing clean?" Terra's mind was returning to her now, along with a large dose of suspicion.

"Our sins have dirtied it." The women said this in unison, which seemed more than a little creepy to Terra.

"What sins were those?" she asked as she approached the bucket of clothes. Looking at them, she saw they were covered with pale-pink stains—stains that might have been blood.

"We took each other's virginity, foolish us." The woman with the darkest skin said this, her perfect flesh a rich, royal blue.

"Evil us," said the one with the palest skin, hers halfway between white and blue.

"Naughty us," said the one with the cornflower-blue skin.

"You aren't coming on to me, are you?" Terra asked.

The women began to caress one another, running their fingers through each other's waist-length, richly blue hair. The pale-skinned one laid a kiss on the darkest one's neck, and the woman in the middle placed her hands on each of their hips and took turns kissing each of them on the lips—long, passionate kisses that made Terra almost want to join in. No, she *did* want to join in, and she found herself walking nearer, not even realizing how close she had gotten until her hand was almost touching the back of the dark-blue woman. "No!" she yelped, leaping back. "No, I'm here as a cleaning lady, and nothing else. After all, it is my job."

"Who cares to work when they can play?" asked the three women.

"Also, just so you know—three women speaking in unison is kind of creepy, not sexy."

"Curses!" The pale-blue woman pounded the ground with her foot. Terra wasn't all that surprised when it shook a little, but it still scared her a fair amount. She ran over to the clothes and grabbed a dress from the pile, dipping it in the river's flowing water, rubbing together the two sides of its stain. She focused all the magic she could on getting rid of the pink stains...and surprisingly soon, it was spotless. But the three women were slowly stalking toward her, and so she dropped it on the rocky shore and dove for the next dress. That one was soon clean as well, but she still had one to go, and the women were getting very, very close. She yanked the third one out of the basket, dunked it under the water, and it almost flew out of her hands, threatening to flow downstream, along with the last of her hope of ever leaving this place.

She caught it just in time, and, soon enough, it was added to the pile of clean dresses. And then she watched the three women, watched as they turned into three very ordinary-looking women, still with blue skin, but women now without the gorgeous, lithe perfection they had possessed up until that moment.

"Bitch," one of them muttered. Terra didn't bother to pay attention to which one it was.

"Pay up. Let me drink the water."

"Fine," another one grumbled, sounding to Terra like she was getting ready for a long sulk.

"Follow us," said the three women, their voices sullen and empty of even the slightest touch of seduction. So Terra stood up and started walking behind them. It wasn't bad that she felt a little self-satisfied that she had resisted their temptation and kicked their sorry asses at their own game, was it?

They walked across the stones until they reached a fountain, one that would have been pretty damn expensive in the real world—because Terra was strangely certain it was made entirely of diamond. "Now what?"

"Drink, of course."

"Duh." The woman who said this crossed her arms and huffed at Terra, who smiled a little and turned back to the fountain.

She cupped her hands and scooped up some of its water, bringing it to her lips, and drank it down. As it flowed past her lips and down her throat, something began changing within her. Her clothes were drying at a very fast rate, the water running down her skin and onto the ground, where it formed a puddle and then evaporated completely. "What just...what the hell, you three? Did you do something to me?"

"No, you idiot," said the middle-hued one. "*You* did something to you."

"You drank our water," said the dark-blue one, "and now you have almost infinite power over water. Just like us."

"If you have infinite power over water, why was I the only one who could get your clothes clean?"

"Must have been something lame," said the pale-blue woman. "Like true love."

"Guess I'll have to try that the next time I do the wash at the mansion," Terra joked. "A cup of true love instead of laundry detergent."

"Now go," the three women said, and one by one, each turned on her blue heel and stomped off.

Terra was alone once again and had absolutely no idea how to get back. But the river was only a small stretch away, and she did have power over water now, so did that mean she could have the water take her back to her car, wherever it was?

"Worth a try," she said to the emptiness around her. She walked up to the water's edge, dipped in a toe, and then walked into it up to her waist.

"Take me back to my car," she said. And it did.

CHAPTER THIRTEEN

When she walked back up the bank, she was bone-dry after she'd taken only five steps away from the water. *Freakin' awesome!* But what awaited her back at the car wasn't awesome in the least. All four tires on her car were flat, and the acrid smell of burnt rubber filled the air. She threw open her car door to check on Onyx, who was cowering and shaking on the floor. "Onyx! Are you okay, sweetie? What happened?"

"Don't...know...I'm just scared. Very, very scared. I think there was a fire, and some...don't know."

Terra scooped him up and held him to her chest. "It's safe now, Onyx, you're safe now. I've got the power of water now, and I'm sure it can fight off whatever burned those tires." She rubbed his belly until he started to purr softly, and soon he was asleep. She placed him in his seat and got in on her own side, beginning to think. What was she going to do about her car? Her only transportation, now with no ability to move? Perhaps... yes, it was just crazy enough to work.

She took the car jack and tire iron out of the back of the car and removed each of the now-useless tires. Then she held her hand out over the edge of the bridge, watching in delight as water flowed past her hand and around the four areas where the tires had just been. The car began to rise, and she heard a small yowl from the inside of the car, followed by a flash of black fur. Onyx was now hiding behind her legs. "What are you *doing*, Terra?" he asked, his voice trembling.

"Just fixing our problem, that's all." She was grinning by now, and she let out a little gleeful laugh. This was fun! "Look, Onyx, now we can keep going. Isn't that cool?"

"I guess…I guess it *is* cool. But is it safe?" He slunk out from behind her legs and walked up to a tire, sniffing it cautiously. "Smells like…fish."

"I'll bet it does. Now, let's get in and keep going. Only two parts of the quest left, my cute little kitty-friend."

"You sound a little too excitable." Onyx sniffed. "Cool your jets."

"No, someone else's jets need cooling, and it's not me. Whoever the bastard was who ruined my tires, *that's* whose jets need cooling."

"All I know," Onyx said, hopping into the car and settling into his chair, "is that I'm pretty sure I don't want to run into whoever it was. I singed my fur on a candle once, and I don't want to experience the full-body version."

"I'm sure we'll be fine," Terra said, starting up the engine. The car started rolling—or flowing? Terra thought—forward across the bridge, and it seemed to be moving even more smoothly than it had with the rubber tires. Terra was sure they'd be fine, or at least mostly sure. She couldn't help but feel just a tiny bit worried, but she was too busy paying attention to her recent success to pay much heed to that little bit of fear.

❖

The three blue women lay in ruins. The man with flaming horns was almost to the well, almost ready to complete the next part of the quest. But when he reached the well, he found it was dry, with not even a drop left in its basin. He got ready to scream out his rage, to burn every tree within a hundred miles. He should have done more than burn the car's tires, he thought with immense fury...and really, he *would* have done more, but something seemed to stand in his way.

He wouldn't let *this* stand in his way, though. He would just steal that stupid warlock's power, steal it like he'd stolen the power of his family, the power that had given him his other form, this horned creature of fire. He could easy kill Saturn as he slept, and it wouldn't take him long to locate his scent and catch up. After all, night was falling soon, and that was when his power burned the brightest.

❖

Terra had continued down the road that started after the bridge, and the woods were starting to grow a little bit darker when she reached a small road to the left.

A handmade, wooden sign at the beginning of the drive said FOR TERRA on it, with an arrow pointing to the left—pointing to wherever the road led. Was she supposed to believe this was really for her? After what had happened to her tires, it very well could have been a trick—or worse. There was only one way to learn if it was, though, so she turned onto the driveway and followed it around a few turns, arriving at last at a wooden cottage. It didn't look especially evil, and it was as good a place as any to spend the night—much better than in her car, at least.

She got out and stretched, and watched as Onyx did the same, his stretching showing far more flexibility than she happened to have. If only she had a bit more flex in her body... Athene surely wouldn't complain if they could try a few new positions. Then again, magic could help with that, so...but Terra shook her head. Who cared about more flexibility when you had magic dildos, right? She looked toward the cottage, only about fifteen feet away from her car. "This place seem safe to you?" she asked Onyx.

"Safer than your car's tires were." He walked up to the house's porch and climbed its three steps, then jumped onto a wicker rocking chair with a faded brown cushion. Onyx sighed happily. "Now, I think I'm going to take a little nap before supper. You still have some of that canned food for me?"

"I don't think so, Onyx, but maybe we can find some food in the cabin." Terra started to reach for her overnight bag, but... did she really need it now? After all, if she could change her clothes now through magic, why did she need that bag? It only held stuff she'd already worn, anyway. Not that she knew what she was doing with her new powers yet, not really, but maybe she could figure out a thing or two before bed. She was just happy she didn't have any more driving to do. "Stay put," she said to her new tires, and then she followed Onyx up the steps and opened the cabin's screen door.

"You should probably come inside with me," she told Onyx, who slowly opened his eyes and yawned. "We don't know who burned the tires, and we aren't near any water. I still don't have the hang of this magic stuff, you know."

"Oh, do I *ever*. But I suppose you're right." Onyx jumped down from the chair, following her to the door. "Is it even unlocked, though?"

She tested the doorknob. Damn it all—it was locked. "So much for going i—"

The door swung open then, so suddenly that she almost fell over. "What the fuck?"

In front of her stood a raccoon or, actually, *sat* a raccoon, because it was on the back of a stag. "What the fook indeed," said the raccoon, in a distinctly British accent.

Terra took a deep breath. "I guess...I guess I shouldn't be all that surprised by talking animals, not by now. Though I wasn't really expecting company at this cabin. I'm Terra." She shook the raccoon's paw as gently as she could. But how on earth did you shake hands (hooves?) with a deer?

"Pleased to make your acquaintance, Terra. Not that we animals di'n't already know your name or what you're here for, missy. Your mum warned us about everything that will transpire this night."

"My *mom*? You knew her?"

"Yes, we did. Many years ago, or perhaps twenty-two, she told us she was with child, and you would be needin' *our* help in about twenty-two years. So, we hung around here, played some chess, mated with each other when we were bored, and now, here you are, missy, and here we are, too. Name's Freddy, by the by, and my steed is Uther. You'll have to excuse 'is complete and utter lack of manners—'e's a rude one, this stag."

"Oh, shut up, Freddy. I'm not nearly as rude as you, you pernicious little nipper."

"Ain't a single bone in my body that's pernicious, and I only nip when it's called for. Like now!" The raccoon—Freddy— bared his teeth and growled at the stag, but instead of biting him, he patted Uther on the head and leapt down. "I suppose you'll be wantin' some information, so if I was you, I'd see if I had anything to drink to help me along my information-searchin' way."

"How did you know about the wine?" Terra wasn't sure whether she trusted these creatures yet, as likeable as the two of them seemed. Not that she couldn't hold her own against a petite creature like Freddy, but the stag would probably be a bit more of a challenge. "And why should I trust you two?"

"We knew about the wine because of your mum. She said you would bring some and that you would need it to see somethin' important. Do you 'ave it or not, li'ul lamb?"

"Little lamb? *Really?*" But Terra had decided that the two creatures didn't want to harm her, or they would have attacked by now. "Yeah, I have some wine. It's supposed to show me my future, or something like that. I don't know if it works yet."

"I've been off the drink since those vomit-inducin' thimbleberries we fermented and turned into juice, so the wine's all yours. But I would recommend having a nice meal first. My wife and I fixed you some supper, and it's just about ready. She made some delicious cilantro flatbread, and for dessert, we'll be eatin' some spotted dick."

"You do know you just offered a dish with the word 'dick' in its name to a dyke, don't you?"

"Yes, my wife Lizzie thought it would be amusing. Bit rude of her, aye?"

"It was your idea, ya dumb fook," came a voice from inside the cabin.

"I'd be coming inside soon if I were you, missy. It's not going to stay cold out forever. I can feel something very 'ot and very angry comin' towards us. And our protective circle is only around the cabin."

"Protective circle?"

"Your mum told us to get one set up. You ain't the only one with a bit of magic to you. Now get your cat, get your wine, and get inside, you 'ear?"

The stag nosed the door open wider and said, "He's right, you know. He may be a stupid, good-for-nothing, masked bandit, but he's right."

"Shut up!" Both Freddy and Lizzie yelled this, but they cackled right after shouting at Uther.

"Think we should trust them?" she asked Onyx quietly as they walked back to her car.

"I think so. Didn't smell anything off about them, other than a lack of proper bathing from Freddy."

"You rude little thing. Such a snob." Terra nudged Onyx with her foot, but she was laughing as she did. She got the wine out of the car and made sure she had her doorway stone, too. She decided she might as well bring her bag, too. Then she went inside. Onyx rushed in next to her, almost tripping her as he raced through the front door.

"I suppose a lock isn't necessary?"

"Oh, that door is always locked to everyone but us critters," Uther said, nuzzling against Terra's side. "You smell nice—like apple pie and powerful magic. What a yummy combination. Can I nibble on your hair?"

"'e's just kiddin', the stupid thing. I'n't that royt, ya big antlered freak?"

"Kidding? I guess I was." Uther laughed or, Terra thought, snorted.

"You guys are just a bunch of troublemakers, aren't you?"

"Who ya callin' troublemakers, missy?" Another raccoon, presumably Lizzie, said this, looking at Terra with surprisingly intelligent eyes for a raccoon. Then Lizzie turned back to the pot she was stirring. That must have been where the delicious smell had come from. A spicy and full-bodied scent had been tickling Terra's nostrils since she'd gone inside.

"Are you making Indian? I thought you were just making flatbread and spotted dick, whatever that is." Terra took a moment to examine the room now. Large windows were in every wall, through which she could see the trees close to the house and the ones a bit farther away. Something seemed to be making everything about ten feet away from the cabin a bit blurry. Was the magic circle causing that effect?

She turned her eyes to the inside of the cabin again. In the back were five large beds, each with a beautiful, multi-colored, checked quilt. Closer to her and to her left was what must have been the living room, with four armchairs, a short, leather couch, and two large bookcases near the window, filled with at least half as many books as Athene had in her bedroom library (half as many still was very impressive). Terra saw *The Call of the Wild* and a number of volumes of Shakespeare on its very top shelf, along with a large sampling of Vonnegut and at least six *The Far Side* comic collections. The thought of these forest creatures enjoying *The Far Side* brought a smile to her face. Or at least a wider smile, because she was really enjoying Freddy, Uther, and Lizzie's company. They really were charming, she thought, and rather funny, too.

The kitchen section of the cabin contained a large, six-burner stove, an equally large fridge, a wall of upper and lower cabinets, and a long, rectangular table, surrounded by over a dozen chairs. Bowls, plates, silverware, and glasses sat at each place. One spot alone held a wine glass. Terra guessed that one was for her.

A question had entered her head, though, and she just had to ask them. "Is it just me, or is this place bigger from the inside?"

Freddy walked over to her and stood on his hind legs, placing his paw on his nose and pointing the other at Terra. "By Jove, she's got it!"

"Rude, Freddy, rude and uncalled for. Just like always. But I loves ya all the same. By the way, Terra, love, supper's ready. Would you care to call in the rest of our family, Uther?" Lizzie let go of the spoon that was in the pot and climbed down from the stool she'd been standing on. "They're all excited, you know. They've been wantin' to meet ya."

"I guess I'm looking forward to meeting them, too." Terra pulled a chair out from the table and sat down, placing the wine and the doorway stone on the table and her bag by her chair. This would be interesting, meeting all these critters—these *talking* critters—who apparently knew all about her. Who knew all about her and had been expecting her, too. She hadn't been expecting them, nor did she know what to expect.

She hoped they could explain all of this, because to the best of her knowledge, her mother hadn't been psychic. That wasn't a trait witches and warlocks ever had. Instead, it always belonged to other types of magical folk. Onyx could occasionally predict things, but not anything big. Once, he had known that the mansion would be getting a mouse infestation, with a few hitchhiking inside a load of hay for the horses. He had tried to warn Athene, who in turn had tried to warn her parents, but they refused to believe he'd known, even after the mice were dashing across the various floors in the palace and getting into their pantry's expensive food stores. Onyx had been delighted, though, that they hadn't done anything about it. He was at a rather unhealthy weight until the ten cats the Werths finally brought in to take care of the problem caught the mice. Not a single one of the cats was male and gay, to Onyx's chagrin.

Terra was wondering, now, if in some way her mother *had* been able to predict the future, and if so, what that said about her daughter. And then the door to the cabin opened, and in came a young woman with ankle-length, white-blond hair and a warm, fuzzy-feeling-causing smile. Or at least that's what it did to Terra, because she instantly knew that this woman was a kindred spirit, a thought she'd had only one other time, when she'd first met Athene.

"Hello, Terra. I am Woodbyne, and these are my friends." The woman walked—or floated, almost—over to the table and sat down next to her, and what seemed like an unending stream of animals entered the cabin. There was a fox, a badger, two dark-brown squirrels, a skunk, a mid-sized black bear, another stag, a mountain lion that started purring when it locked eyes with Terra, and a bobcat with beautiful dark-green eyes to match its grass-colored fur and shiny, emerald-colored spots.

"An honor to meet you," the fox said, in a deep, rich male voice. "Please excuse us if we wait to sit down. We never dine until we take on our nighttime forms. And if your mother was right, we will be requiring them tonight."

"'Nighttime forms'? What does that mean? And you'll be requiring them, too? Is that…is that because of whoever melted my tires?"

"Ah, so you have come across the evil being your mother warned us of. I am relieved that you are all right, young Terra." The fox walked up to her and put its front paws on her knee, seeming like it was trying to look right into her eyes. "You and the cat will take heed and stay indoors tonight. That is an order."

"Hey! I don't really like being ordered around all that much, Foxie. Especially by a creature I could totally take in a fight."

The fox growled a little at that, but he lost the staring contest, being the first to look away. "I will post our two biggest warriors by the front door then. It is almost as important that we keep you in as it is that we keep him out."

"Him? So the thing that ruined my tires is a 'him'?"

"To the best of our knowledge, yes. That was all your mother knew—that he would have power over fire and that he would be male."

"What else did she know about tonight?" Terra's stomach growled loudly after she asked this question, her hunger drawing her away from her interest in an answer. It was just as well, because she didn't get one, not one of the animals offering any kind of response to what she had asked.

"We will be changing soon enough," said one of the squirrels in a quiet squeak of a voice.

"Yes, within the next thirty seconds, and please do excuse our nudity."

"Your…nudity? Aren't you already naked?" Terra was becoming curious as to what these "nighttime forms" would look like, but as the fox began to stand on its hind legs, and as its fur began to recede, she found that he, and the rest of the animals, were all turning into large humans. The fox became a muscular man with red, chin-length hair, and the two raccoons, Freddy and Lizzie, became a man and a woman of similar heights, both with rich-brown hair, although the man's was shorter and had a bit more curl to it than the woman's. He also had a few more wrinkles than she did, smile lines surrounding each of the brown eyes set in his round, forty-something face.

She watched as the rest of the animals changed, the two squirrels becoming short, redheaded female twins, the badger an amber-skinned man, the skunk a tall, statuesque woman. And then, after everyone else, Uther the stag changed. His antlers shrank a fair amount, but didn't disappear completely as he grew taller, and taller, until he towered over Terra.

"Should we eat, then, Miz Terra?" asked Freddy. "By the by, it is a large pleasure to meet you in the—shall we say—flesh." He began to laugh uproariously at his joke, tilting his head back as he did, and Terra frowned slightly as his whole body began to shake with his undeserved laughter. Instead, and as politely as she could, she suggested that they maybe go and clothe themselves so they could all eat. A second loud growl from her stomach made Freddy laugh again. Instead of teasing her, though, he and the other people went over to various closets around the bedroom area of the cabin, taking out clothes and getting dressed.

Once they were all fully clothed, they sat around the table and Lizzie served up the thick, red curry and pieces of the warm, fluffy bread, flecked with green herbs, which she'd taken out of the large oven. Then the nighttime-formed people all joined hands and bowed their heads, Woodbyne taking Terra's left hand and Lizzie taking her right. She took their lead and bowed her head as well.

Surprisingly, Freddy was the one who spoke. "Our dearest father and our dearest mother, we thank you for givin' us life, givin' us breath, givin' us fur, and givin' us our nighttime forms. We thank you also for Terra, the one who is destined to stop him, and the one whom tonight we will protect. We ask that you 'elp us in our fight, and we thank you for givin' us faith to do as we 'ave and to do as we will. Now, everyone, dig in!"

Terra opened her eyes, which had become a bit moist from Freddy's words. It seemed he wasn't all machismo and rude words after all.

Dinner was delicious. Terra had never had curry before, and while she found herself drinking glass after glass of water, she still finished her first bowl and then immediately asked for seconds. Luckily, Lizzie had made four pots of it, so there was more than enough to go around. The bear, or Nicolai, as it turned out he was called, ended up having fourths, but everyone else was content with two bowls, some only one. Woodbyne was the only person who didn't eat, instead drinking a glass of some sort of green, swirling liquid that didn't really look all that appealing. Especially not compared to the curry and the delicious, chewy bread.

She asked Woodbyne what her drink was, and the woman merely smiled and shook her head. Then Terra's jaw dropped a little as the woman's lovely, long hair began to float out behind her, rippling in some sort of invisible breeze. The young-looking woman lifted her hand to her left ear, the one that faced the front door, and seemed to be listening to something quite intently. "They say he will be here a little past midnight. We will ready our weapons while you visit your lover, Terra."

"How did you know about that?" Her words came out much sharper than she intended them to, so she cleared her throat, then said, "Sorry. I mean, you all know so much about me, and I know pretty much nothing about any of you."

"We are the forest." Woodbyne's voice was quiet but steady as she spoke. "We are all the leaves and trees, all the dirt and moss, and all the ones who call it home. We are all of it, and we will keep you safe."

"I guess that *kind* of explains it. And I'm guessing that's the best I'm going to get out of any of you guys."

Freddy laughed, pointing his finger at her. "She's a smart one, this li'ul gal. Jus' like her mum, she is!"

"Thanks, Freddy. So, I suppose I'm not going to hear any more about this mum of mine, either?"

"No, ma'am, not hearin' but you may be seein' instead."

"Whatever the fuck *that* means, you little bastard."

"Hey, don't you call me li'ul." Everyone laughed at that, even Onyx, who had cute touches of thick, white cream on his face from his dinner. Terra glowered at Freddy for a few moments until she gave in and started laughing, too. He might have been a bastard, but he was damn likeable. Damn funny, too.

"So," Lizzie asked once the laughter had died down, "'ow is it that you visit this girlfriend of yours, bein' so far away from 'er?"

"It's this thing called a doorway stone. You'll see me using it as soon as I find an appropriate door."

"Try the one in the very back of the cabin. You can use it the normal way later. That's where the loo is." Lizzie got up from the table and began taking the dishes to the sink. "Now, Freddy, you don't 'ave to get to all of them tonight, but make sure the pots are soaked at the very least."

"Yes, *ma'am*." Freddy pecked her on the nose and ran his hand over her head, and she nuzzled him in return, looking more like her raccoon self than her human form as she did this.

Terra got up from the table and took her doorway stone with her, placing it in front of the door she'd been directed to, located in the very back of the cabin. She knew swimming right after a big meal wasn't recommended, but she didn't think the same could be said about sex, and she had other hungers that needed sating this night.

Chapter Fourteen

When Terra stepped into Athene's bedroom, it was shockingly different from usual—almost entirely different. Pale-colored lanterns were hanging around the room, and they cast a sensual, red tint across every surface inside it. Instead of the queen-sized bed she was used to, a large, round platform stood in the room's center, on top of which lay a flat, silk-covered mattress, the fabric a rich crimson color, and it looked like it would be incredibly soft to the touch. Next to it sat a delicate lacquered table, and on top of that was a white, ceramic bowl full of black liquid (ink?) and a large Japanese paintbrush.

As her eyes adjusted to the light, Terra glanced around a little, looking for Athene. Then she felt two hands running up her sides. She jumped a little at the sudden touch, and a voice—Athene's—said, "It's okay, Terra. It's me, your lover." Her voice was soft and sweet, like honeyed liqueur, its smooth, rich sound flowing over Terra's bare skin like the softest of silks.

Athene began to unbutton Terra's vest, her hands brushing against her breasts every few moments. Next, she pulled Terra's T-shirt over her head and then unhooked her bra, dropping each item on the floor beside their feet. Then Terra's pants were added to the pile, along with her shoes. Last, her panties came off, and then she felt Athene press her own naked skin up against her bare back, Athene's hard nipples and chest brushing against her skin as she cupped Terra's breasts and pulled at her nipples.

"Fuck!" she growled only moments later. Athene had just pinched them in unison. But each pinch was more than welcome, and her limbs went soft as her nipples became hard. Athene continued to play with them in this rougher-than-usual way, pulling at them and rolling each one roughly between her thumbs and forefingers.

Athene's lips were now on her back, kissing her softly—first a gentle kiss on her right shoulder blade, and next one on her left. "I have a surprise for you," she told Terra in between kisses. She was silent for a moment. "But you have to be blindfolded. Are you willing?"

"Totally." Terra's answer came out like a soft sigh; she was already melting against Athene, the warmth from her body heating up parts of Terra's own, parts desperately in need of some pressure, desperately in need of release. She almost asked Athene if she could get her off then and there, but she was rather curious about what would happen to her once she was blindfolded, so she held her tongue

"Good girl," Athene said, sounding like she was smiling. She walked a few steps away from Terra, coming back a few moments later. "Bend down a little," she told her, and Terra did so, sighing again as a silken, black blindfold was placed in front of her eyes and tied behind her head. "Follow me." Athene took her hand, and she began to lead her forward, seemingly in the direction of the round bed. Was that where the "action" was to occur? And there the bed was, pressing against her thighs. Athene's gentle hands guided her onto it, and she pulled Terra onto her back and slowly spread her legs apart. She felt Athene's hand on her cunt then, and Athene's thumb brushed lightly—

far too lightly—against her clit. "Please, more pressure." She had never been too proud to beg for pleasure, and now was obviously not the right moment to change her ways.

"I have something else in mind, sweetie. Sorry to disappoint you." Athene's hand moved away from her body, and Terra grunted out her disapproval at its removal. Especially the part of said hand that had been touching her clit. She was about to complain, but, "I need it for the paintbrush," she heard Athene say. Well, this was likely to be at least a *little* bit interesting. She heard the quiet sound of liquid splashing against something; she guessed it was the sound of the paintbrush being dipped into the ink.

"You saw the ink, Terra?"

"Yes."

"Just making sure. Good. I...I want to tell you something, now," she said, and a drop of the ink fell in between Terra's breasts. She gasped at its coldness, but moments later, it began to heat up, bit by bit, until she began to tremble from the warmth of it as it slowly flowed across her skin. And her trembling increased as she began to feel something else—the ink was making her skin tingle, tingle and pulse, and she felt the same sensation on her cunt and nipples, a sensation that went a far way past mere pleasure. "This isn't just any ink." Athene sounded proud of herself, and, Terra thought, she sure couldn't blame her. "It's special, and I made it just for you. It's supposed to send heat to all the right parts of your body," Athene said, and then the brush was gliding down the crevice between Terra's breasts, her whole body shuddering for a few seconds as the ink heated up and the skin it touched began to tingle—her clit and cunt doing the same. "It's going to send pleasure to all the right parts of you," Athene said. Well, duh, Terra thought, and then she pretty much ceased to think, because now she was getting closer...yes, so much closer...to coming.

As the brush continued to glide down her body, over her bellybutton, past it and to where her mons pubis began, her cunt clenched, tightened, more and more, until the brush finally found its way to her clit. Once there, Athene teased her, circling the brush around her clit's outer edges, circling it until she finally let the brush reach Terra's most sensitive, most pleasure-inducing spot. Terra began to come in waves as it touched that spot, the brush steadily building pressure as she gasped, then moaned, then screamed, her body quaking and twitching and shaking as the orgasm bloomed and kept growing, still more...still more. She clenched the mattress's soft sheet as the orgasm continued to control every single bit of her body, and pretty much all of her mind, and a hard splash of liquid flowed down her cunt's lips, hitting every inch of the space in between them, drops of it even entering her, fucking her hole like a dildo might, filling her up until she screamed she couldn't take any more.

A second later, her body grew completely dry, and she collapsed to the bed, still shaking and gasping as she came down from coming so hard. She was almost about to melt, her body was so relaxed, so very loose and calm.

"That was..." She took a deep breath. "Holy fucking hell, that was nice."

"Lift up your head," Athene said. She did, and Athene untied the blindfold and took it away from her face, and Terra gazed into her eyes. She felt an immense amount of love for Athene as she looked at her, love just as intense as her pleasure had been only moments ago. Love that could almost make her come again. Athene leaned down then and kissed her, just once, on the lips.

"Thank you," Terra murmured when Athene pulled away from her, and she spent a little while longer gazing into her beautiful, blue-green eyes. "Thank you."

They talked for a long while after that, and then Terra said she had to go. "You know how much I would love to stay here. I would love to stay here forever, just like this. But I have to go back to my cabin. I promise I'll come back tomorrow, though."

"Or perhaps I can come to you?"

"That sounds terrific. You can come to me…and with me, too, I hope."

"And after I come *to* you, and before I come *with* you, how about I come *on to* you?"

They were laughing a little by now, but their laughter changed to sad silence as Terra stood up and got off the bed and started to put her clothes back on. "I wish I didn't have to go."

"Me, too. Me, too, Terra."

But she left, after giving Athene a long kiss good-bye. She turned back once as she left and saw the room shimmering around Athene, whose lovely, sloping back was turned to the door Terra had just opened. Athene's bedroom began to change then, back to how it usually looked, and Terra heard a quiet, sad sigh as she eased the door shut behind her, now back in the cabin once more. Back in the cabin and far away from Athene.

CHAPTER FIFTEEN

It was nine o'clock when Terra got back into the cabin, and as she looked through the room, she saw the forest people all drinking some sort of liquid from tall, silver glasses. "What are you all drinking?" she asked, walking over to where they were standing.

"It's to help accentuate our power. A potion handed down from the ones who made us...a gift from our mother and father." It was Woodbyne who told her this, turning her silver eyes toward Terra as she spoke. She didn't look playful, and her eyes didn't have the kindness they had contained hours before. Instead, her face was hard, and her gaze held nothing gentle, nothing peaceful. No, her eyes were cold, and though she smiled at Terra as she looked in her direction, the smile was tight-lipped, and it wasn't exactly believable.

"'e may have friends, after all," Freddy said, taking a long swallow from his glass after he spoke. "Friends or creatures and beings 'e's gained power over. We'll be needin' all the 'elp we can get, yessir."

"You still unwilling to stay inside?" Uther's face was cold as well, and his antlers seemed to have grown a bit in size.

"No, I guess I'm okay in here. I have that wine to drink, and I'm guessing it'll knock me out cold once I've downed the bottle. I'm not used to having more than a few glasses."

"Oh, my dear, that wine doesn't make ya drunk," Lizzie said. "It might make ya wish ya were, though."

One by one, they filed outside, and each of them picked up something near the door—all weapons, except for Woodbyne's tall, gnarled staff, covered in pale-green moss and taller than she was. Her hair flowed out behind her, lighting up the area outside the door as she left the cabin and shut the door behind her.

"You nervous, Onyx?" Terra reached down and stroked his fur, and he pushed back against her hand, his body tight as could be.

"Oh, yes, Terra, very nervous."

"Well, what do you say we get this party started right now?" She hoped the joke would lighten their mood a bit, but as she walked over to her bag and took out the wine, nothing about her mood was the slightest bit light. She wasn't looking forward to seeing whatever this wine would show her. What if it was bad? What if something horrible was going to happen to her, perhaps even tonight?

She had to drink it, though, so she grabbed the wineglass from her spot at the table, untouched until now, and pulled the cork out of the bottle. She was surprised when the glass proved to be somewhat bottomless, as the whole bottle of wine seemed to fit into its cup. Terra raised it, watching the light from the ceiling's hanging lamps turn the wine garnet red and the slightest bit translucent.

"Bottoms up, Onyx," she said, and then she brought the glass to her mouth and began to drink. As it poured through her lips and down her throat, it burned a little, like it was stronger than most wines, more like vodka, or something even harder. The last drops flowed from the glass and into her mouth, and then she dropped it to the table, gasping a little as she fell into her chair.

A few minutes passed, and then a few more, and nothing seemed to happen. The room looked the same, and although her throat still burned a bit from the wine, she didn't feel different, and she certainly wasn't having any visions.

"Well?" she yelled at the room's ceiling. It seemed like the right direction to yell in, as didn't higher powers and beings always come from above? "What the hell are you waiting for? Show me my future!"

Apparently, someone was listening. Terra's eyes shot shut, and then she was watching a hallway from above. A man was standing near a doorway, and he had large, flaming horns, and then Terra noticed another person there, one who was floating and enveloped in flames. She watched for a while, and then she realized something—the person on fire was her, and she knew, in that instant, that the Terra below her was close to death, only moments away from dying, in fact, and it was probably already far too late to save her future self.

"No! No! Stop!" Terra-from-above screamed this out, but it didn't stop, and she watched as she felt the Terra below her dying, more and more of her life force burning to ash in each passing second. Then the room began to grow dark, and all Terra could feel was fear, immense pain, and the closeness of death.

Her eyes shot open. She was gasping for breath, her skin sticky with sweat, her eyes watering and burning a bit. But she was back in the cottage, and she wasn't on fire, wasn't dying. Everything was back to normal.

"Motherfucker!" was the first thing Terra thought to say. She slowly got up from the table, her legs shaking, and Onyx dashed to her side.

"What is it, Terra? What happened? Are you all right?"

"I...I don't know. I saw a man, with horns—horns that were on fire—and I was beneath him, and I think..." She lowered herself onto one of the beds and lay down on its edge, placing her head on one of its fluffy, white pillows. "Onyx, I think I was just about to die."

"Motherfucker!" Onyx yelled. Then he jumped up onto the bed. "Nope, yelling that didn't help me either. What…what do you mean, about to die? Like, for sure? And where were you? And what did his face look like? And how were you going to die?"

"Slow down, little guy, slow down. I don't know who he was, or where I was. I think it was dark, and big…it was indoors, I think, with very little light coming in. Just the fire from his horns and the fire he was holding. The fire he surrounded me with. Oh, Goddess, Onyx, what am I going to do?" She reached out a shaking hand and ran it down his side, mussing up his fur as her hand jittered back and forth. Her hand shook less the second time she stroked him, and by the third time her hand was steady.

"I think…I think I should just go to sleep, Onyx. There's nothing I can do about it right now. First, though, I'm going to use the bathroom door in its usual way, and then I'll change for bed." She got her toothpaste and toothbrush out of her overnight bag and patted Onyx on the head on her way to the back of the cabin.

Once Terra was in the bathroom, she realized she had nothing to wear to bed. The forest folk were fine with her seeing *them* naked, but she wasn't really comfortable with them seeing *her* that way. So she'd have to figure out something in terms of clothes. After she'd washed her face with the soap by the sink and brushed her teeth, she decided to take off her clothes and picture herself in pajamas. Maybe that would work?

She got naked for the second time that night (it wasn't *nearly* as much fun this time) and closed her eyes. A few seconds later, she opened them, tentatively, and yep, she was wearing a pair of cotton shorts and a tank top, both black with white clouds floating across them—literally, because the embroidered clouds were moving across the cloth, some of them with rain coming from them, and one where the moon was just starting to peek out from behind the cloud's shimmery gray shape. "Wicked!"

She couldn't wait to show Onyx, so she bounced out of the bathroom and headed to the bed where she'd left him. But he was out cold, snoring softly and twitching a little as he slept. He looked so happy sleeping there that Terra couldn't talk herself into waking him, even to show him her totally awesome new PJs *that she'd made herself.* Soon, she felt a yawn coming on, so she yawned wide and loud without covering her mouth, and then she climbed into the bed. She hoped she wouldn't wake up with someone in it next to her—especially Freddy, although he seemed pretty darn taken and very in love with his wife. She also hoped she would sleep through the night, and with that, all thoughts of what the forest folk and the horned man were up to, and even thoughts of her vision of the future left her head. Only a little while after her head hit the pillow, she was asleep, but it seemed she'd only been asleep for a few minutes when something woke her up.

"What?" Terra mumbled at the sudden disturbance, still halfway in dreamland. She rubbed her eyes and slowly sat up. "Who's there?" she asked, and then she gasped when she recognized the glowing form in front of her. "Mom? Mommy? What are you doing here?"

Her mother laid a finger to her lips and whispered, "Shh."

"No, tell me, please, Mom. Why are you here? Am I...am I still asleep?"

Her mother's eyes slowly opened then, and they were bright, glowing, and red. Fire danced and leapt inside the whites of her eyes, and Terra knew then that this wasn't her mother, and that her life was in danger. What was she supposed to do? And was this threat, this false vision of her mother...was it in her dreams or in reality?

"Go back to sleep. Go back to sleep!"

Terra couldn't fight its order—the being's power was much too strong. She lay back down and got ready to close her eyes. She didn't want to, she wanted to stay awake, but she was so, so very tired. But somehow, she managed to keep her eyes open, just a little, and she watched with fear as the woman who wasn't her mother began to grow flaming horns and start walking toward her.

"Get back," Terra whispered. Then her arm whipped up into the air—had *she* done that? "Get back!" she shouted, in a voice that was not her own. Bright-green light shot out of her hand and hit the horned being, and it screamed and shook and then turned and ran, shrieking as it did.

"I'll find you, wherever you go! You can't beat me, you pathetic little warlock! No one can!"

She wasn't sure if she was safe now, but she was so very tired, and so she climbed back into bed, her dreams full of half-animal, half-human creatures playing music and taking turns leaping over a bonfire while their singing voices rang out into the moonlit night.

Chapter Sixteen

Terra was relieved to find that the only things sharing her bed when she woke in the morning were two squirrels and Onyx, the squirrels both sleeping with their heads on his stomach. What a cute sight—if only she had a camera! Then she could torment Onyx with the photo for the rest of their lives.

But how long would that be? she wondered, as memories of her night began to return to her. That dream, well, she found herself thinking that if it had indeed been a dream, it also probably had held real power, and real risk. And whatever power had saved her that night might not be there the next time she needed it. Where had that powerful light come from? Not from her, because her final words to the horned being had not shot from her lips in her own voice. She rubbed the sleep out of her eyes and pushed back the covers, getting up out of bed and heading to the bathroom.

It seemed to be unoccupied, so she went inside and turned on the faucet, splashing some cold water on her face. She doubted there would be coffee. Magical forest animals wouldn't need coffee, would they? Even if they were in human form half of the time, they probably woke up with the sun's light, nothing else required. She dried off her face on a lovely towel with a dark-green ivy pattern and left the bathroom, heading toward the kitchen and the smell that was probably part of what had woken her. It was a lovely smell, like cinnamon, sugar, and freshly baked bread, and she found the two raccoons sitting at the table munching on some meat and seeds. She saw some thick toast at her spot, buttered and with cinnamon and sugar sprinkled on top. Next to the toast were two fried eggs and some berries, which she guessed had come from the surrounding woods. And what do you know, she spotted a mug of what looked to be steaming-hot coffee. Terra sat down and reached for the mug, full of gratitude for the caffeinated beverage.

"Mornin'." Freddy had been holding Lizzie's paw with his free hand, but he reached that one up in greeting as Terra approached the table. "Ya sleep like the dead, li'ul lady."

She shook a little at his words. "Don't say that."

"Oy, I apologize. I guess last night was 'ard for you too, eh? We managed to scare the big fooker away, but 'e almost got to ya. Ya can thank us later, missy. But not wit' sex, as I'm taken."

"Shut up, ya big fat fool." Lizzie smacked Freddy on the arm. "Miz Terra's got 'erself scared, didn't ya? We may've scared the 'orned beast off, but we di'n't warn the poor girl enough. We apologize, Terra." She smacked Freddy again.

"Yes, Terra, we both do." If raccoons could look affronted, that was how Freddy looked right then, but there was a touch of embarrassment to his face as well. Terra hoped he was embarrassed for teasing her, and not for having to apologize.

But she had more important things to consider than whether he meant what he'd said—like whether forest animals made good coffee. Terra took a big gulp from her mug, burning her mouth a little. But oh, was it worth it. The coffee was just perfect, and the rest of the meal hit the spot just right, too. As she ate, the other animals joined them, one by one. Most of them stood next to the table, but the squirrels jumped on top of it, as did Onyx. Terra decided not to mention the cute sight she'd awoken to, instead telling everyone about the dream she'd had—or whatever it had been.

"That wasn't a dream," Uther said, once she'd finished.

"No." Woodbyne was in the same seat as the night before, and she placed her hand on Terra's arm as she said this. "The words that left your mouth—that was the forest, and the light was it as well." She flinched a little as she removed her hand, and Terra saw that her arm was pale green at the elbow, and she had what looked like burns on her chest as well.

"Woodbyne! You're hurt!" Terra felt instant regret that she had let them protect her and, that in the process, her new friend had been injured. A glance around the room showed that the other animals also had wounds. Uther had a cut near his left cheek, and Lizzie's fur was singed all the way down her left shoulder. "I'm so...I'm so sorry." She began to cry, her body shaking a little as the first tear slid down her cheek.

Woodbyne cupped Terra's chin. "You were not ready to face him yet. Your mother thought that would be the case. And we weren't ready either. But the forest—it likes you, Terra. It showed that last night, when it came to your rescue. He had made his way through us and had reached the cabin, and we couldn't stop him. The forest...it saved us all. We will be giving our mother and father an offering right after you leave."

"I'd like to give them an offering, too, if they're the ones who created the forest."

Woodbyne smiled at this, her smile as bright and glowing as the sun coming in through the cabin's windows. "You needn't do that, Terra. And besides, you aren't like us. You are a witch, not a forest dweller. You can't talk to our father and mother."

Terra ate the last bite of her toast and wiped her mouth on the napkin she'd used the night before. "I should be going now, I think." But she sighed at the end of that sentence. Although

Woodbyne's words had stopped her from crying, she felt like she might start all over again at the thought of leaving this cabin and these charming creatures—these charming creatures who had fought for her life.

She packed up her things and walked over to the cabin's door, Onyx at her heels. She paused there, her hand on its knob, and turned back toward the animals. "I should leave all you guys an offering, too. I never even thanked you for what you did."

"You don't need to, Terra," said one of the squirrels.

"Your mother already did," said the other.

"You all never told me about her, actually. Not a thing, really. What was she like? How did you know her? And how could she see into the future?"

"You'll know soon enough, Terra," Uther said. "She told us that, too."

After one last good-bye, and a leg-hug from each of the raccoons, she left the cabin and got back into her car. The water tires were still there, but the car's hood had what looked like burn marks on it. Terra ran her fingers over them; they were still warm.

"I hope the Jag runs okay with those," she said, getting in on her side.

Onyx climbed over her lap and settled into his seat. "I'm sure it will. I bet your new friend the forest made sure of it."

"My new friend? Silly, being friends with an ecosystem." She gave the cat a small noogie and started the car. It seemed to run just fine, the engine purring like it always did, so she pulled away from the house and back onto the driveway.

Once they were back on the main road, it didn't take long before it became pavement. Terra had turned on the radio, and she was singing (and Onyx was yowling) to "Yellow Submarine." The song was just getting to a good part when Terra noticed for the first time that Onyx was sitting on something that didn't match the car's leather interior.

"Onyx, what are you sitting on? What the hell is that?" She quickly pulled over to the right and turned off the car, yanking Onyx into her lap. Where he'd been lying, beneath a light dusting of white cat fur, was a jacket, a jacket made out of material that matched the cabin's dark-green bathroom towels exactly.

"I believe it's from Woodbyne, based on the fact that she told me that last night when she came back inside the cabin. Will you *please* put me down now? I was enjoying the music. It was just getting to my favorite part."

"What's the deal with it, then?" Terra put him down, but picked up the jacket before he had time to settle onto it again— or the chance to get more cat fur on it. "It's pretty, and it looks like it's my size, but other than that, does it serve a use?"

"It's protection, she said. Wear it and you'll be safer. That's all I know. She was tired when she told me, and so was I. I insist you turn the car back on—right now! I don't want to miss the rest of the song."

"Fine, you whiny bugger, we'll get going again. Right after I put on the jacket." She picked off most of the cat fur and then began to slip into it—it was a perfect fit. It was also slightly cool against her bare arms. And it smelled good, like the woods she'd just left, mossy and rich. "I guess I get to take a bit of the forest with me."

"I guess you *do*." Onyx was sulking now, but soon he was happy again, singing even louder than before as the song drew to a close. And then some very familiar notes came on, as the next song started up.

"You bastard, you cursed us!" Ringo was singing the same words he'd sung only about six minutes ago, and they were treated to his charming voice again and again for the next fifteen minutes.

"Make. It. Stop." Onyx sounded miserable by the...what was it now, Terra wondered—the tenth time they were hearing it? The hundredth? However many times it had been, it had been far too many, and they both breathed a loud sigh of relief as one of Terra's favorite Ramones songs started playing next instead.

"I've never liked punk much," Onyx said, "but anything is better than hearing that horrible song again."

"Don't tempt the car to play it again. Seems like Athene put in a fail-safe—or something—to make sure we would get along during this trip."

"I'll have to talk to her about that when we get back." Onyx didn't sound like he merely wanted to "talk."

"You could talk to her, or we could tie her up and make her listen to 'I Wanna Hold Your Hand.'"

"I'm guessing she wouldn't only be hearing the song once?"

"No, more like twenty or so times."

"Sounds like the ideal punishment."

The radio seemed to think that they were getting along again, because instead of the Ramones, the next song was Pink Floyd, and the one after that was U2. Terra and Onyx went back to singing and howling along with the music—and, more importantly, they went back to *getting* along.

Chapter Seventeen

They'd been driving for about three hours when Terra spotted a fast-food restaurant by the side of the road. "I'm starving, Onyx, how about you? Maybe I can get you a burger sans bun and accoutrements?"

"Yum" was all Onyx said. Terra took it as a "Yes, please," and she parked in front of it, then got out of the car, stretching before she went into the restaurant. It didn't appear to have a drive-through, so she had pulled into a spot in its almost-empty parking lot. Only one other car was there, and when Terra saw it was the one Pan had been driving when she last saw him, she couldn't help smiling. She also couldn't help looking forward to seeing her fellow queer member on the completely stupid quest.

Inside the restaurant, rainbow flags were everywhere, and Pan was, surprisingly, behind the counter in full drag; he wore a sequined gown and a large, bright-blue bouffant. "Thought I'd have some fun," he told Terra with a grin. "How do you like the place?"

"I just *love* it. Any chance Onyx can come in? I didn't know you'd be here, Pan. It's great to see you!"

Pan came out from around the counter and gave her a hug. "Sure, of course Onyx can join you!"

Terra went outside and told Onyx about the restaurant. She couldn't help noticing that he sounded a little wary when he told her he was going to join her inside. Nor could she help noticing his hesitant tone when he asked her, "Are you sure this is the real Pan we're dealing with?"

"Why, Onyx, what's gotten into you? Why so doubtful?" She picked him up, carrying him through the restaurant's front door.

Onyx leapt out of her arms and said, "Just don't make me say 'I told you so.'"

After a delicious lunch of a chicken burger and some sweet-potato fries, Terra thanked Pan and left the restaurant with Onyx. "See? Nothing to worry about. Nothing at all, you silly cat." They got back into the car, and Terra started the ignition. And then things started to get weird.

Instead of being in the car, Terra was walking through a field, straight toward a bed where Athene lay. "What are you doing here, Athene?" she asked. "And what happened to my car? The restaurant? All of that?"

"Pan contacted me, and we set this up together," Athene told her, as she flowed into an upright position. She was wearing black silk cuffs on her wrists and a matching silk garter belt, which held up her dark lace stockings. On her feet were shiny (and immensely sexy, Terra thought) black stilettos. As she watched Terra watch her, she spread her legs, giving Terra a lovely view of her cunt, a cunt that already looked ripe for the fucking, all of it wet and flushed a lovely, rich pink.

"So, is this real?" Terra had to ask. But before she could get an answer, she noticed her own clothes changing hue and shape and texture, and moments later, she was wearing a full, latex bodysuit. As the suit spread across her body, she also felt a dildo and a plug appearing inside her, filling up her cunt and ass. They shifted a bit (in a *very* pleasant way) as she walked up to the bed. She climbed onto it, her crotch now incredibly close to Athene's pussy, just mere inches away.

"Not exactly real, no," Athene said, trailing a finger down Terra's chest and stomach. She stopped right at her crotch, and Terra felt slight tingles from her touch, tingles that were delicious and delightfully arousing.

"What is it, then?" She pushed up against Athene, flattening her down to the bed, and watched in surprise as Athene's wrists and ankles became attached to the bed. Now she was completely restrained, and this seemed to make Terra's cunt decide that it needed to throb a little at the sight. As it pulsed, the dildo and plug shifted inside her, slowly moving in and out of her holes, and then, wonderfully, they began to vibrate, and she would have soaked straight through her bodysuit if it hadn't been made out of rubber.

"It doesn't really matter where you are, does it? Since I'm here, with you?" Athene looked at Terra's face, an inquisitive expression on her own, then asked, "This isn't...upsetting you, is it?" As she waited for her answer, she arched up from the bed and ran her tongue up Terra's neck, stopping right where her lips began.

"No, it isn't. Not at all. It's turning me on a whole fucking lot, though." Something started pressing in between them, then, and Terra realized the dildo inside her had somehow grown, that it was now much longer, perhaps twice as long—only it had grown away from her body this time, and the part that wasn't inside her was now inside Athene. She leaned down a little, intending to kiss Athene, and then she found her own wrists had become wrapped in silk, and she too was attached to the bed. She tested her restraints, grunting softly as they pulled her hard against Athene's body. Then things got a whole lot better. The double-ended dildo began to move back and forth, between them, and somehow the plug in her ass had grown in length as well, and now they were both getting fucked in both holes, the plug and the dildo sliding into Athene and a little out of her and then back, the butt plug doing the same. And, of course, that meant they were sliding a little into *her* and then back, too. She wasn't even close to complaining about this turn of events, but everything had been mildly startling so far...startling and arousing, of course.

So what could Terra do but kiss Athene, hard and rough, her lips showing Athene that she might have been bound to the bed, but she still had teeth, so to speak. Then she used her non-metaphoric teeth to nip at Athene, digging them into her lower lip just a little as she noticed the dildo and plug speeding up each back-and-forth movement. Athene gasped from the first bite, moaning into Terra's slightly open mouth, and it seemed as if Athene's moan was vibrating all the way down her body, and all the way through it, until her every cell was quivering and aroused.

"How hard can you take it?" Athene asked, then, and the items that were penetrating both of them paused, almost expectantly, perhaps. Was Athene in control of them? Was she the reason they were getting fucked so well? Was she the reason Terra was so aroused, so incredibly turned on, and so incredibly close? And did it even really matter? No, not in the least. All that mattered was that she was on top of Athene's lovely, soft body, and they were both getting fucked...quite well, at that. And all that mattered was that she was close, and that she could tell, almost for sure, that Athene was close, too.

She stared down at Athene, then, locking eyes with her, just as they were locked together, the restraints holding them against one another and the dildo and the plug connecting them, their cunts and asses filled equally full. Terra blinked, licked her lips, and then told Athene, "Give it your all—give it... fucking...everything." She'd only just said the last word when the dildo and plug began to pound into her, to slam back and forth between her holes and Athene's. Her body was pulled even closer against Athene's, the restraints yanking her down until she was pressed tight against every inch of her lover. Then her catsuit disappeared, and now, just like Athene, she was wearing nothing, nothing at all. Her wet hole and its juices were exposed to the air, and they were also exposed to the lovely body beneath her. She placed her lips on Athene's, whispering, "Thank you, thank you..." again and again, as she kissed her again and again, as the dildo and plug fucked them, fucked both of them over the edge and each into her own powerful orgasm. Their mouths were pressed together as they came, and Athene's cries and moans shook against Terra's mouth, Athene's own pushed open and full of Terra's tongue.

The ties on their bodies loosened then, and their arms were freed, and Athene pulled her even closer, holding her firmly in her arms. "I never want to let you go, Terra," she breathed into Terra's ear.

"Me either, me either," she replied. Terra meant it fully, completely, with every single bit of herself.

Just as suddenly as the field and Athene had appeared, they disappeared. But Terra wasn't back in her car. She was in the middle of the desert, sitting on a camel in a saddle, and Onyx was sitting in front of her. "What the fuck?" she yelped, almost falling off the large creature. Onyx yowled in shock, his voiced displeasure seeming to show that he'd shown up there right as she had.

"This is crazy!" she shouted. "Where the fuck are we, anyway? And how did we get here?" Terra gasped as the beast beneath her made a strange bellowing sound. But even stranger than the sound was the fact that it seemed to be trying to communicate something.

"Sorry, I don't speak camel," she told it, patting its neck. "Do you speak English, by any chance?"

The camel huffed and then snorted.

"Apparently not." Here goes nothing, she thought, for what seemed like the thousandth time since she'd left the mansion. She closed her eyes, wobbling back and forth a little as the camel continued to move forward, and she squeezed its hump for good luck, wondering yet again if her newfound powers were up to her latest request of them.

It seemed to work, as warmth spread through her body and traveled down to her fingers.

"Stop that—it tickles!" said a low-pitched woman's voice. The words seemed to have come from the camel.

"Hey, it worked!" Terra patted the camel on the hump, grinning as she did. This magic stuff just seemed to be getting easier and easier.

Now that she felt more at ease, she began to take in her surroundings, feeling a little more secure now that she could communicate with the animal carrying her and Onyx across the land. Sand dunes spread out as far as the eye could see, and the path they were walking along seemed to be well traveled, footprints and what must have been hoof prints going in both directions. They were moving upward, having reached a quickly rising part of the path, and she hoped that meant they would arrive somewhere with water soon, because hell, was she *ever* thirsty.

Looking down at her body now, she saw that she was dressed in harem pants, and after touching her head, she learned that she was wearing what seemed like a turban. She was still wearing her magic jacket, thankfully. Unlike her car, it had made it this far, and she was more than happy to see it again. After all, the jacket might wind up coming in handy. Hopefully it wouldn't become necessary, but considering all the surprises on her trip so far, it might, especially with the fact that for all she knew the evil creature with flaming horns might be close behind. Or perhaps a little ahead of her, instead. She sent out a brief prayer that he was nowhere near at all, but she couldn't help thinking there was a large chance he was. She began to pet Onyx, hoping to calm her nerves with the soft, comforting feel of his fur.

"That feels goooood," he said, and began to purr almost as soon as he was done speaking.

"So, camel, what's your name? And where are you taking us? We're in a desert, so is this where I'm supposed to make it rain?" She had just remembered that part of the quest—the third part. She didn't know how she was going to make it rain, although some part of her seemed to think she had a way to do it. Annoyingly, the thought didn't go much further than that.

"I'm Shudun." The camel's voice came out flat, but with a hint of a smile riding on her words. "My name means *powerful*, or *straight*. You happen to be only one of those, if I am correct."

"No, I'm not straight…but I'm not especially powerful, either."

"Oh, I *highly* doubt that." The camel shook a little beneath her, and Terra realized she was chuckling softly as she carried them up the hill.

"You didn't answer my second question, Shudun." She still couldn't see what was over the hill, and although the camel seemed nice enough, there was no way to tell whether it was carrying them somewhere good and useful, or bad and, possibly, dangerous.

"I don't have to, because look—we're here."

And wherever "here" was, Terra thought to herself, yep, they had just reached it, because they had also reached the top of the rise. Beneath them was a market, made up of many tented tables and stalls. Each and every table was crowded with glass bottles, plastic bottles, and see-through containers of all types and sizes. As they approached the market, the people were calling out words in many different tongues, all of their voices rising into the hot, dry air.

They all seemed to be speaking different languages, and they were all different races, wearing different types of colorful clothes. One man in a turban and long flowing robes yelled out a word in Arabic over and over again. For some strange reason, Terra knew exactly what he was saying. "Water! Water here!" he cried out each time. A delicate-looking woman at a red-and-black stall, wearing a similarly colored kimono, yelled, "I have the best! The best water! Come to me, friend! Come to me!" in Japanese, another language that Terra certainly didn't know much of. "A number of others shouted "Water!" over and over again, in all different languages, ones which Terra happened to know all of a sudden. They included Cherokee, German, Greek...and many, many others, Terra realized as she looked down at all the people offering her their "wares."

"Here's my water, it seems," Terra said. She followed these words with a loud sigh. She may have liked to have multiple options in life (except when it came to girlfriends), but this? This was just *ridiculous*.

Chapter Eighteen

As she (somewhat clumsily) got off the camel, and helped Onyx down next, Terra couldn't help but wonder again how on earth she had wound up here. It was also rather strange, the way she'd managed to make it to each of the necessary spots so far for the quest's four tasks. Would the fourth location prove to be as easy to find, though?

She reminded herself that she hadn't even completed the third task, and she felt that—despite being in the middle of a hot, sandy desert—there was far too much water available in this particular part of it. Perhaps she could find some to drink, first. But what if it was poisoned or had unexpected qualities? What if it turned her into an ostrich, or took away her ability to speak? What if...what if it made her forget about Athene and the quest?

She shuddered at the thought and tried to brush it away, doing her best to concentrate on the job at hand—finding water for her and Onyx to drink and then finding water she could use to make it rain here, in this dry, desert wasteland. Rain sounded especially nice at the moment, as she was sweating and then some, her body practically drenched and her clothes almost entirely soaked through. She started down the path to the stalls, and once there, she let her eyes travel down the space between them all—goddamn, was it *ever* long!

But then she remembered—she had an affinity for water now. She could control it, make it do her will. Would her ability work here? *Only one way to find out.*

And so she and Onyx walked down the wide, straight, strangely empty area between the stalls, Terra's sandaled feet stirring up the dusty ground in front of them. After they'd passed a number of stalls, she stopped walking, raised her hand, and closed her eyes. Concentrate—she had to *concentrate.*

In the beginning, she thought of her thirst, thought of the feel of silky, sweet, fresh, ice-cold water cascading down her throat, caressing it and filling it with coolness and relief. Because drinking some water, some nice, fresh, cold water, well, that was almost as appealing as sex at this moment in time.

At the thought of sex, another part of Terra started getting wet, of course—that mere hint of sex made her think of Athene and herself, drinking from large goblets of the most delicious water available, both of them in a cool, small, chest-deep pool made of silver-flecked marble, the water almost as soft as Athene's skin as it touched her back and ass and thighs. She would down what was left in her cup and then wade over to Athene, boost her up out of the water and onto the sun-warmed, tiled edge of the pool. Then she would spread Athene's lovely legs...and then she would make one very special part of Athene's body even wetter than the rest of it, licking the slippery spot between her legs as droplets of water ran down her thighs and trickled down her cheeks as she ate her out. Athene would come, quick, almost too fast, and then it would be Terra's turn.

Instead of sitting on the tiled edge of the pool, she would float on her back in the crystal-clear water, with her cunt half in and half out of the water. Athene would eat her out for a bit, her chin and body submerged as she lapped at her pussy, and then she would gently pull Terra's relaxed body underneath the flowing fountain that fed and refreshed the pool; she would help lift her legs up over the edge until the fountain's water hit her in the exactly perfect and most pleasurable spot. And Athene would hold her up, teasing her breasts, pulling and twisting her nipples—hard, rough, angry pinches, twisting them back and forth with a large amount of pressure. But that wouldn't stop her from coming, it wouldn't slow down her impending orgasm—she would come almost as quickly as Athene had, and she would…

Terra's attention returned to the market. Her eyes shot open as she came, her body shaking as the orgasm traveled quickly through her body and across her sweat-covered skin.

She looked down as the orgasm ended and saw her hand wrapped around a bottle of water, glass with a rubber stopper, topped with a wax seal that showed, upon closer look, a woman drinking from a goblet in miniature.

"How much?" she asked the full-figured, gorgeous Indian woman standing in the stall in front of her—in the stall where the bottle must have come from.

The woman was blushing a little, her eyes averted. "Viewing your pleasure was payment enough. You may have it, and then you will see why I am famous for my drinking water." The woman's accent was as beautiful as she was, and Terra watched with a touch of interest as the woman swept her glossy, black braid behind her shoulder and reached for the bottle. "Please, miss, allow me. Water this fine is meant to be drunk from only the finest of goblets."

Terra handed the woman the bottle and watched as she uncorked it and poured it into a black stone goblet in the back of the stall. She then handed Terra the goblet, and Terra drank the water. It was the most delicious liquid ever to have touched her tongue.

It tasted of many things. Honey, cinnamon, strawberries, chocolate, and wine were the first flavors she detected, each of them coming one by one. Then she tasted compassion, kindness, freedom, and sensual pleasures given with love. Lastly, she tasted love itself—immeasurable love, of the kind you could experience only once in your life, if you were truly lucky. She tasted Athene then—every bit of Athene's voice and words…her touch…her smile when looking at Terra's face. And, "Oh!" Terra gasped, because that proved to be the most delicious taste of them all.

"Thank you…thank you so, so much." Terra handed the goblet back to the woman. She wanted more of that water, but something that delicious, that perfect, could become addictive, and besides, she had the best part of its tastes at home. She had it in human form, back in Athene's bedroom. And she would have that "best part" soon enough. All she had to do first was figure out a way to make it rain. All she had to do. Yeah, *right*.

"I am impressed," the woman said as she took the goblet from Terra's hands. "Many have tasted this water, and all of them have had too much of it. They have become lost in its taste and its power. How are you able to abstain, miss?"

"I can because I have it at home. No, I have something even better than it at home."

"Yes, oh yes, I see now," the woman said with a quiet smile. "You have love written across your skin. True love. I see now," she said again.

"Now," Terra said, picking up Onyx, "you can have some less-dangerous water, and then we'll make it rain."

"Oh *joy*. Rain, a cat's favorite thing. And hey, why can't I have some of the special water?"

She almost said "Because you don't have someone waiting for you at home," but that felt far too cruel. Onyx seemed to figure it out on his own, though. He sighed and told the woman, "Give me your tastiest *plain*, non-magical water. Apparently I don't have the necessary qualities to handle the hard stuff."

The woman poured some water into a small stone bowl, and Onyx lapped it all up as quickly as his little tongue could move. He sighed again once the bowl was empty, but this sigh was a happy one. "That water...oh my God...best ever. I'd give you five stars if I could, but I'm guessing you don't want to show up in our local newspaper back home."

She chuckled softly at that. "No, I don't. Besides, my stand doesn't have a name, nor does it have a regular location. It only appears with the rest of the stands whenever a traveler needs water of the magical variety. Like you, miss. Now, I believe my business is done for the day." The woman turned away from them and walked to the back of the stall, her lavender-and-green sari flowing back and forth in a slight wind that had just started. "Good luck, miss," she said over her shoulder. The wind picked up, getting stronger and stronger, and then the woman's stand lifted off the ground and began to fly off, rising higher with each passing second, becoming smaller, too, until it was merely a spot in the far distance. Terra blinked at it once, and when her eyes reopened, it was gone.

"Wasn't that interesting?" She scratched Onyx's head, and he nuzzled her palm.

"And wasn't that water just *wonderful*? Mine may not have been magic, but its deliciousness almost seemed magical. I wish the water at home was that tasty."

"Onyx, you get fresh-from-the-bottle Italian spring water! You have it good, dude. I wouldn't complain if I were you. Some cats have to drink out of rain puddles, you know."

"G-ross! Ick! Fine, I feel beyond blessed in that case. Now, isn't it time for me to get soaked to the bone? Let's get this over with, shall we?"

Terra scanned the remaining stalls, and then she realized only one was left. When had the rest disappeared? Had they blown away with the woman, when she blinked, perhaps? How the hell had she missed the mass exodus? "Wow, they're all just...gone, Onyx. Where do you think they went?"

"On to the next person who deserved to find them, I suppose. Looks like you only have one left to choose from. You better pray it's the right one."

She felt a strong pull then, and visions of rain clouds began to show up in her head—rain clouds gathering and then pelting down rain. "No, I think this is the right stand. I can feel it, kitty-cat. I just...somehow, I just know."

"Onward, then, toward the horrors of rain and, even worse, soaked fur. Will you please put me down now? I'm going to hide in the stall once it starts raining, and hope it doesn't fly off into the sky and join the others."

"I don't think that's such a good idea." She furrowed her brow, then glanced to the left and held her hand out, pointing to a flat plot of sand about twenty feet to their left. The air began to shimmer there, visible ripples appearing in the air, and then they were followed by a quiet popping noise, and a large, scarlet tent appeared. On its front was a surprisingly solid-looking cloth door that had a little square flap at the bottom of it—a kitty-door, perhaps?

"That should keep you dry, I imagine." Terra felt a little touch of pride bloom within her chest. Pulling that tent out of thin air had been pretty damn awesome, if she did say so herself.

Onyx climbed out of her arms and landed on the ground with a small *thump*. He took off running, practically bounding in the direction of the tent. "Catch you later, Terra! Thanks bundles, you lovely, lovely lady!" In what seemed like seconds, he had dashed through the door and into the tent. She hoped the inside of it had turned out okay. She'd meant for there to be a bed of some sort, and a small pillow for Onyx. Then, with one final push of power, she tried her best to give him a bowl of chicken and a bowl of water. She heard what sounded like, "Yum, food!" from inside of the tent. Apparently it had worked!

Now, Terra thought, it was time to get very, very wet. And not in the good way. If only she'd thought to bring an umbrella.

Chapter Nineteen

Terra began to walk toward the stand, each step carrying a surprising amount of confidence and calm. She was far past merely guessing that this was the right stand, but she couldn't help but wonder what the price would be for *this* water? Would it be impossible to afford? What might it wind up costing her?

But when she reached the stand, she saw Zeus standing inside. He was dressed in a long white toga, with a braided gold rope wrapped around his waist and crisscrossing his chest.

"Zeus? What are you doing here?"

"I just had some free time on my hands, thought I'd stop by and see how the quest was progressing." Zeus crossed his arms. "The real question, Terra, is what are *you* doing here? What is a woman doing on this most important of quests?"

Shit, Terra thought. If only she'd changed herself back after she'd left on the quest! But how could she have known that she'd still need to be in disguise? And how on earth could she have stood having a hairy chest and man hands throughout the last few days, anyway?

"*Especially* a woman of low birth, one of our...cleaning ladies?" Zeus scowled as he continued, and those last words seemed to be dripping with distaste, maybe even disgust.

"Hey, man, I made it this far. Now let me have my water. I need to make it rain, and I'm pretty sure I'll be able to pull it off. I may be a woman, and I may even be a cleaning lady, but I also love your daughter with all my heart. So, if you don't mind…" She had reached the stand by then and noticed that only one bottle sat on its surface. It was burnished gold, with small, unfaceted rubies imbedded in the metal, and it appeared to have no stopper.

"We'll see about your ability to pull it off, young woman. And we'll see if you'll be able to finish the quest, too. I seriously doubt it, because the last part, the last task, is definitely, by far, the hardest. I don't even know how you've made it this far, a woman with such weak powers! You could barely make your *mouth* wet with your magic!" He laughed hard and long at what Terra thought was a rather unfunny joke.

"We'll see about it, indeed," she growled, and she lifted the bottle off the table and took a long pull of water from its opening. But she didn't swallow it. Instead, she spit it out into the growing wind, the mouthful of water spraying from her lips. Some of it, to her great delight, hit Zeus, and she smirked at him as a grimace spread across his face. She also might have watched with a fair bit of joy as he tried to flick the droplets of water off his clothes.

"Look!" she cried out, because it had worked! The sky was growing thick with dark, rather ominous-looking clouds, and soon, not a single speck of blue sky or sun could be seen. The air became cold quite suddenly, and the wind was now at least twice as strong as it had been a few seconds ago.

"Good," Terra said, her voice a low rumble, a low rumble echoed by the booms of thunder from less than a mile away. She looked down, just for a moment, and saw that her body was glowing, a glow echoed by flashes of golden lightning in the surrounding desert.

A small drop of water hit her arm from above. Then another. Then another, another…another!

"It's raining, old man, it's raining!" But Zeus and his stand were gone, and Terra couldn't help feeling a little glad that he was no longer there. She felt even gladder that it was raining— rain *she* had made fall there, where she stood. So this was what the other Magic Ones felt when they used their strongest powers. It felt amazing, to be this powerful. No ordinary person could make it rain, after all; she was ordinary no longer. Now she was one of *them*.

The rain kept coming down, harder and harder, and she spun under the pelting water, round and round, drinking it all in, figuratively and literally, the water slightly warm and full of life as it touched her tongue. After a few more minutes, she'd had her fill, and besides, she was starting to get a little too cold, a little too wet. So she fought her way back to the tent through the downpour, opened its thick cloth door, and then fought like mad against the wind until she finally managed to shut it behind her.

"Hot damn, that was amazing!" She grinned at Onyx, who looked wide-eyed and shocked.

A wave of immense tiredness overcame her then, and so she stumbled over to the bed, barely taking in the beautiful, multicolored silk fabric draped all around the tent's interior and also canopying the bed. No, she was too tired to think much other than "Pretty, pretty silk," which she mumbled as she collapsed onto the mattress. It was the last thing she thought as she fell into a deep and heartily deserved sleep.

In her dreams, Athene came to her and told Terra her magic jacket was not from the forest folk, but instead from the man who had been chasing her. She should take it off and burn it, cleanse it with fire.

Terra awoke a while later and felt slightly overheated, almost like the fire Athene had been talking about in the dream had actually licked across her skin as she slept. But should she take off the jacket? She looked down at it, at its lovely forest pattern, and she brushed her fingers across its soft, supple cloth. It didn't feel bad—like it was evil—but who was she to say? So she took it off and placed it in the corner of the tent. Maybe the real Athene could tell her what to do about it when they next met up.

But when *would* they next meet up? What was Athene doing right then? Athene's last visit had been hours ago. And a peek outside told her it was dark now: night had fallen in the desert. It was colder, too, especially with her jacket off, now with only a loose, silk tank top to keep her upper body warm. She shivered and then realized she didn't have to be cold. A wave of her hand created a thermostat on the wall near the bed, and she turned it up to sixty-five—a thermostat seemed safer than a fire. Despite what the Dream Athene had told her to do with the jacket, she couldn't help feeling a little fear at the thought of fire, fear probably brought on by the creature with the flaming horns who had melted her tires and tried to kill her when she was in the forest. No, if she had to destroy the jacket, she wouldn't use fire, no matter what Dream Athene seemed to think.

Terra wanted to see Real Athene now, but she didn't know what she would come across were she to enter her bedroom at this moment. Who knew what time it was back at the mansion, and who knew whether it would be Athene in her bedroom or someone else...perhaps a guard, or even one of Athene's parents. The last thing Terra needed was a meeting with Cer in Athene's quarters, something that had almost happened one night in the not-so-distant past.

She had been sneaking down the hallway toward Athene's room when Cer had started coming down that hallway from the opposite direction. She'd gotten a sudden glare on her face, almost like she'd seen Terra, and she'd glanced from left to right while Terra hid behind the wall where a door led to the outside. The door had been propped open slightly, the cool night breeze making her aware of the sweat that had begun to form on her skin—sweat that came from the terrible thought that Cer would catch her, catch her and then send her from the mansion, and Athene's life, for good. Athene had told her that Cer wanted only the best for her only daughter, but it was clearly she who decided what—and whom—that "best" consisted of. So there would be no trip to Athene's room, not right now, not out of the blue like this.

Terra realized then that she had placed the doorway stone by the door to the tent while she'd been thinking all of this. "What the hell?"

Then the door began to open, and she glanced around, looking for some kind of weapon. A pair of hands grabbed her shoulders as her head was turned, but they were gentle, familiar hands—the hands of a beautiful woman whom she happened to love. "Athene! Don't scare me like that! I almost clobbered you with...with a pillow!"

"I don't think that would have done much damage to a would-be attacker, sweetie. But if you want to have a pillow fight, I suppose I'm game."

Terra pulled Athene into her arms and squeezed her tight against her. "I'm so glad to see you," she said, her lips against Athene's ear. "I didn't know when I'd see you next, after that last meeting in the vision, the last visit we had."

"Did you enjoy yourself? I just had to see you, and I wanted to try out some new magic. I hope you weren't driving when we met up. I didn't know a way to figure out what you were doing when I pulled you into the vision."

"I kinda was," Terra said, pulling back slightly so she could look into Athene's eyes, "but then, after the vision, I was here, in the desert, on a camel! And then it seemed like it was time for the next part of the quest, I guess. You didn't have anything to do with the camel I was riding on, did you?" She scowled slightly, looking down at Athene with fake distrust.

"You almost sound suspicious, sweetie." Athene's brow furrowed slightly, but she smiled when Terra laughed.

"No, no, not suspicious, just confused. All of this has worked out surprisingly well. I don't know how the rest of my competition is doing on this quest, but I hope I'm at least slightly close to the lead."

"My father has a map where he follows the progress all of you are making, and it seems that you, Zou Jin, and Eros are in the lead. Each of you has completed the water quest, although it seems that Eros...well, something looks a little off about how he's completed each part. To me, not to my father or mother. They're both rooting for Eros, it seems. His family is very powerful, with strong magic and loads of wealth, to boot. And I think my parents believe we'd make a good match. Which would be fine, if I were straight and attracted to assholes."

"I wanted to ask you about something, actually, before we..."

Athene grinned. "Sure, as long as it doesn't take more than a few minutes. I just can't wait for us to..." She nudged Terra suggestively as she spoke, and Terra laughed a little.

"Did you...did you bring me a dream just now? About my jacket from the forest folk?"

"I don't even *know* about a jacket from the forest folk, sweetie, or about forest folk, and I didn't bring you a dream about either of those things, whatever they are. If I were to bring you a dream, it would be a dirrrty one." She wiggled her eyebrows and looked ready to pounce on her.

"Good. I *think* it's good, at least. I guess I won't burn the jacket after all. But there just so happens to be a fire somewhere else right now, one you're helping to kindle, if you know what I mean. So, maybe we could..." Terra's voice took on a more sultry tone, and she gestured toward the bed.

"What about Onyx? Isn't he in here?" Athene glanced around until her eyes found the cat.

"Oh, I'll take care of that, just a second." Terra walked over to where he lay asleep on his pillow, and she brushed her fingers lightly across his fur, sending some energy into him. She looked up and smiled at Athene. "Now he'll sleep through a hurricane, at least for the next four hours or so."

"Four hours? You seem to have some mighty big ideas in that pretty little head of yours, my dear."

"It's just in case. You know, if you want to go again...and again...and again." She grinned down at her girlfriend, her face clearly showing what she wanted to do in terms of going. "Hey, do you have any good ideas for our time together?" Terra asked her.

"Maybe. Terra, look at all those long ribbons of silk draped around the bed. With a little magic, I think we could do some *very* special things with them and your body."

"Or yours," Terra said, and then she pressed herself up against Athene, and pressed her lips to hers, and pulled both of them down onto the soft, silk-covered bed. Once they were nude, their clothes tossed carelessly to either side of the floor surrounding the bed, Athene sat upright. "You ready to try something new?" she asked Terra, and Terra nodded. The truth was, she could hardly wait.

Athene got onto her knees and reached to the right and left of the bed. She brushed her fingers across two strips of silk, each multicolored and reminiscent of the tropics. Each one began to dance, almost as though a slight breeze was just entering the room. But there was no breeze, and a breeze wouldn't have made them do what they did next—each strip wrapped around one of Terra's wrists, pulling her arms up a few inches off the bed. Then Athene reached back and touched two more, and they wrapped around Terra's torso, right beneath her breasts, and the ribbons pulled her into an upright position. Athene touched a few more, and they wrapped around Terra's thighs, and legs, slowly twisting in the air as they slipped their way across her bare skin.

Now Terra was floating, almost flying, her whole body lifted a few feet above the bed. It all felt wonderful—the feel of the silk, the suspension in mid-air, and especially the occasional brush of Athene's fingers against her skin, Then, next, another piece of silk floated up, but this one drifted away from Terra. Instead, it moved beyond her and went in the direction of Athene's body. Then this piece fastened itself into a dildo-like shape, and shortly after it did, two final strips of silk wound around Athene's thighs and attached the silk dildo to her crotch. She walked across the bed to Terra, and a small thought crossed Terra's mind as she approached her—a thought that it felt lovely to be floating in the air like this, and that she very much wished Athene could experience the same joy she was feeling right then.

Athene had just reached her as she began to think this thought, and the second she brought her hands to Terra's skin, she, too, began to rise into the air, just like Terra had pictured—only she was moving into the air without the help of the silk tethers!

"You're...flying!" Terra grinned, but the look of shock on Athene's face quickly moved her grin down a few notches. "You're...am *I* doing that?"

"You? Yes, I...think you are." The look of shock was beginning to fade, and her features softened into a much more relaxed expression. "Wow, so this is what the birds feel like... completely weightless...completely free." Athene looked fully calmed down as she said this, a serene expression with lowered eyelids and a soft, subtle smile now replacing the look of slight fear that had been there moments ago. "I like this." She sighed. "I really, really do."

"That's a relief. But…I didn't mean to do this, Athene. I was just picturing you up there, next to me, floating like I am— only without the silk holding you up."

"Wow. I mean, Terra, you've grown so much while we've been apart. I think your magical abilities are stronger than mine, now. Maybe even *much* stronger."

"Really?" Terra couldn't help letting her voice—and face— show the joy she felt upon hearing those words. It wasn't that she wanted to be more powerful than her girlfriend; it was just that, after all these years of being so magically ungifted, growing in the opposite direction—far in the opposite direction—felt incredible. No, more than incredible. It felt, to use a silly word (but one that fit exceptionally well), *magical.*

But that thought was soon replaced with a few far more sexually themed ones, as her girlfriend's levitating body settled down atop hers. It was then, also, that the silk dildo began to slip inside her slick, more-than-ready cunt. The silk dildo was the softest thing she'd ever felt inside herself; it met her flesh with the gentlest and most delicate kind of pressure, the gentlest and most delicate of touches. It was gentle, yes, but the sensations it caused still gave her reason to arch her back a little and gasp as its width and length spread her open, as it pushed its way deep inside her, deeper still, until it was all the way in. And then the caresses began, with each small, flowing movement inside her coming from every single bit of the silk dildo's rigid—yet, also, surprisingly pliant—surface. It began to massage the best spot inside her, then—her G-spot—rolling and tumbling and pressing its silken cloth against it, causing little tremors of pleasure and warmth to roll back and forth throughout her entire cunt, and even her torso.

She was so lost in the dildo's actions that it took her a few minutes to notice that the silk holding her midair had ceased to stay still. Instead, now it rippled across her skin, massaging it and kissing it with the push and pull of its fabric. The silk continued to brush her flesh as Athene leaned down and kissed her, too, her lips meeting Terra's as the hips that the dildo was attached to began to roll and rock. Athene's moves brought the dildo into motion, its silk girth sliding in and out of her, in and out and, yes, always massaging her G-spot. Then it began to rub against her clit, too, which almost sent her over the edge. But she (barely) managed to hold out. She wanted this pleasure, and this time with Athene's body, above her...touching her... fucking her...she wanted it to *last*. Maybe not the four hours she'd joked about, but a few more minutes wouldn't hurt, oh, no, no, *no*.

A strip of the silk reached back as she thought this, and it ran its length against her asshole, swirling around it like a tongue might, only even softer, even gentler, almost a tickle of pressure, and always just the right amount of pressure, too. She only hoped that Athene was feeling just as much pleasure as she was in these moments.

Or, maybe, fingers crossed, even more.

Terra knew then, without looking (because her eyes were shut tight) that the silk had taken over now. She knew, somehow, just *knew*, that it was fucking her instead of Athene's hips and body doing the work. And somehow, she knew that some of it was fucking Athene's cunt now, too, sliding in and out of her as well. She just knew it all, without a doubt, and perhaps she knew it because, just as she had made Athene fly with only a few thoughts, she also must have used her magical abilities to make the silk move to her will, also with just the slightest of thoughts. It seemed like it was moving to her will, right now, as it slid in and out of Athene and touched her body in, apparently (and luckily), all the right spots. Just as it was doing to each and every inch of her own pleasure-filled skin.

The thrusts of the silk sped up, and more and more strips of silk slid across their naked bodies, dancing across their skin. Each strip pressed or flicked against all of their most sensitive parts—their nipples, their cunts, their asses and clitorises. The silk's lovely movements also touched their two lower openings, the two that, in particular, were always capable of feeling the utmost pleasure. They were still kissing, though, even throughout all of this. And it was the kissing, Terra thought... yes, the kissing, and not the silk's touches, or its thrusts, that brought her the most pleasure. Because while the silk may have felt good...wonderful...and amazing...each kiss from Athene felt infinitely better. And because each press of Athene's lips against her own made love flow into her body, love that was the ultimate pleasure of them all. It was the thing she was aware of the most in these delicious passing minutes.

And Terra almost missed her release and her orgasm's beginning. She was just so completely lost in the feeling of Athene's lips. But as she came, and as Athene did, too, they joined their lips into one last kiss, each pair of lips locked tight against the other, a kiss that felt like it lasted days, or years, perhaps; a kiss that lasted until Terra's orgasm finally subsided; a kiss that lasted until the firmness of the bed's mattress pressed against her back once more.

The silk tethers slowly slipped off her body, floating back to their previous locations around the bed, and she relaxed into the mattress, relaxed against Athene's perfect, lovely body, and soon she was fast asleep.

Chapter Twenty

When Terra next opened her eyes, a face was looking down at her, a face that was not Athene's.

"Fuck!" She shot into an upright position and did her best to take in her surroundings as quickly as possible. She was still on the bed from the night before, but there was no tent around her, and she was completely naked. A few feet from the bed sat her car, and standing all around her bed were women dressed in flowered dresses and aprons. None of them looked like they were more than three feet in height, and all of them had short, black hair, over-sized feet and hands, and looks of concern on their round, chubby faces.

"Where am I, who the *fuck* are all of you, and where's my girlfriend?"

The woman closest to her was the first to speak. "You are in Herdwicke, our home, and we welcome you here, traveler. We are some of the Hoomes, and we request that you stay with us for a while."

Then Terra finally remembered that yep, she was still stark naked. She blushed a little and pulled her knees to her chest, trying to hide what all these petite women had already obviously seen. None of them seemed the least bit offended by her nudity, but she still rushed to put on the underwear and clothes, consisting of a pair of pale-gray slacks and a white, flowered blouse, which happened to be lying on the bed. They could have been enchanted and able to suck the very life out of her, but right now all she cared about was getting her body covered and out of the view of whoever—and *what*ever—these "Hoomes" happened to be.

"So," she said as she finished buttoning her shirt, "how did I wind up here?"

"We don't know, but we do know that it seems as if it's been awhile since you've bathed." The woman who said this scrunched up her tiny face as she spoke, and Terra felt the flush returning to her face.

The time to be discreet was long past, so she sniffed her armpit, her own face scrunching up as the scent hit her nostrils. "Damn, I smell way too ripe." Terra didn't know how she had managed to reach this state of ripeness. Maybe it had been the heat of the desert? The lovely sex she'd had with Athene the night before, sex that could have made her work up a sweat?

She looked at the woman who'd mentioned her eau de stink and asked her, "Do you have anywhere I can bathe? I doubt your showers would be big enough for me." If they even had them, she thought, because who knew how technologically advanced Hoomes happened to be? She had noticed a well only a few feet away from her, so maybe they didn't even have electricity. They were sure to have one thing, though—magic.

Two of the women came forward and helped her off the bed. "We do indeed," said the one holding her left hand, and for a second Terra thought the woman had read her mind. But she wasn't talking about magic. "We bathe in some pools not far from here, pools surrounded by lavender and flowering ivy. They are especially beautiful, the ivy-flowers, and smell like heaven itself."

"That sounds much better than a shower." Then, she thought to add, "I hope I'll have a little privacy while I'm there?"

"I'll be happy to provide some. I have no interest in seeing you completely naked…again." That was Onyx, who thankfully had made it here with her.

"Of course I wouldn't *dare* to disgust *you* with my naked body, my dear little kitty." Terra patted him on the head.

"You can patronize me as much as you want, just as long as I don't have to bathe with you."

The two women who had helped her off the bed led her down a path lined with trees and a large number of tiny, one-story houses, the perfect size for these Hoomes, but Terra couldn't go inside any of them. They were the perfect size for Onyx but not even close to the right size for her five-nine frame. She'd spent her life feeling tall for a woman, but here she felt like a giant.

About a five-minute walk from their village, they came to the pools the women had told her about. The water looked like it had traveled there straight from the tropics, a clear, beautiful aquamarine that glimmered and sparkled in the sunlight. Surrounding the pools—there were five, Terra saw—were the lavender and flowering ivy the women had spoken of, the ivy growing up the foot-high bamboo fence that surrounded the water. Onyx had followed them there, but he settled down on the other side of the fence, content in cleaning himself the cat way instead of the human way. Terra wasn't jealous of him in that moment, though, as she stared longingly at the beautiful and very inviting pools of gorgeous water.

"I'll get some privacy, right?" she asked the crowd of women.

"Of course," said a Hoome with kind, smiling eyes and graying hair. But that Hoome almost looked a little nervous, too, Terra thought, or maybe regretful. She was so drawn to the pools, though, and so excited at the thought of sliding her filthy, naked body into one of them that she decided to ignore the woman's possible signs of worry. She ignored the looks of nervousness and regret on the rest of their faces, too. Instead, she gazed with a silly smile at the water and waited slightly impatiently for the women to leave. One of them laid a towel by the pool, and another put down a sea-green dish with a few small bars of pale-pink soap in it. Then they all returned the way they'd come, and Terra didn't wait a second before she stripped off her clothes and waded into the water.

It was the perfect temperature, and she found a hollow in the pool's rock sides just the right size for her butt. She closed her eyes and felt herself practically melting against her seat. I'm just closing them for a moment, she thought. *Just a moment.*

But that moment stretched out for much longer than she intended, and soon, she was dreaming.

Her dreams held images of Athene, and Athene was trying to tell her something, something that Terra knew was very, very important. But what was she trying to say? She couldn't quite make it out—it was too quiet, almost mumbled. Something like "For drawing," or "You're drawning," or…what was it? She kept asking Athene to say it more clearly, but then Athene slowly faded from her dream.

Then she was dreaming of a tiger, but it was a small tiger, small and pale, with gray fur and white stripes. The tiger looked familiar somehow, and it was swimming toward her, out in the tropics, and then it reached her and sunk its claws and teeth into her skin.

"Ouch! Motherfucker! Fucking fuck!" Terra shot out of her dreams and shot out of the water, too. She looked down. Dark-red scratches were on her upper chest, and a pale blur of cat was rushing away from her and back to the water's edge.

"You've got to get out of the water!" the cat-blur yelled at Terra. "It's enchanted, the women enchanted it! Get out!"

"How...how do you know that?" But instead of waiting for an answer, she followed his advice, because the cat-blur, otherwise known as Onyx, seemed to truly believe what he was yelling at her. He must have believed it, to have scratched her chest like that—and to have tainted himself by touching a naked human woman. She got out of the pool in record time, her body cold and wet and her mouth full of questions. "What happened, Onyx? Tell me, please!"

Onyx shook himself from head to rear. "I went back to the village when I was done grooming myself, and all the women were gone—indoors, it seemed. But one of the houses had an open window, and I overheard two of the Hoomes. They were talking about a horned man who had threatened them with fire, and he'd told them they had to do away with you or he would burn their homes to the ground and then kill each and every one of them. After that, they started talking about what they were going to do to get rid of me, and so I rushed back here, to wake you up and get you to burn rubber. Oops, please excuse my choice of words."

While Onyx had been talking, Terra had gotten dressed again, not bothering to dry herself. She wasn't too happy about the fact that, in order to get to her car, she would have to go back through to the Hoomes' town, a town full of women who had tried to *kill* her.

She scooped Onyx up into her arms—they would be able to move faster that way—and rushed back down the path. She was pissed, mightily pissed, and a not-so-small part of her wanted vengeance.

But when she reached the village, a few women were standing outside their homes and weeping. They didn't seem to notice her right away, and the one in the middle of them was speaking. It was the woman with the graying hair, and as Terra stood there and watched, she wrapped an arm around each of the other women. "Yes, I know, I know, my dears," she was saying. "We did not want to kill her, but we had to protect ourselves. There was no other way."

Terra's anger dissolved into nothing at those words, and she cleared her throat. The women jumped at the sound, and they all spun around to face her. The Hoomes shared a few very nervous glances with one another, but Terra had just come up with a plan. Hopefully, after she shared it with them, they wouldn't have to be afraid any longer. "I think I might have a solution to the horned man's threat," she said.

"W-what is it?" The woman with the gray hair shook a little as she asked this, but Terra's voice was calm, and as she told them what she thought she could do for them, each of the tiny women's faces slowly changed from terror to apprehension, which finally faded to slight, hesitant smiles.

"You really think you can duplicate it?" asked the shortest of the three women.

"I'm not certain yet, but yeah, I'm pretty sure I can."

About twenty minutes later, each of the women was wearing a miniature version of Terra's magic jacket. She felt a little nervous giving it up, but she couldn't just leave these women here to die, no matter what they'd done to her. She understood how afraid they were of this monstrous man. After all, she'd come face-to-face with him, and she couldn't deny her own fear of him.

As she got into her car with Onyx and drove off, she couldn't help thinking about the horned man, and whether she would see him again. More like *when* she would see him. She really, really didn't want to go up against someone as powerful as he seemed to be.

But a part of her thought that if she did have to battle him, now that she had all this magic inside her, that maybe, just maybe, she would win.

CHAPTER TWENTY-ONE

As she drove down the road from the village of the Hoomes, she hummed the song they'd taught her right before she'd left. They'd said to sing it if she ever needed their help, and they would come to her aid. She didn't want to endanger them again, so she'd decided exactly when and where she'd use the song. Her plan didn't include any danger or threat, unless you included a bit—a *fair* bit—of anxiety and nervousness from her and Athene.

Now a ways down the road, she couldn't help thinking of the man who had threatened first her and the forest folk, and then the Hoomes. She just wanted to complete the last part of the quest and get back home to Athene, and she hoped to avoid coming face-to-face with that evil bastard for the second time.

She came to an on-ramp for a freeway, but she quickly realized it wasn't an ordinary freeway, as when she reached it and got ready to merge, she saw that she was merging into a lane not filled with cars, but chariots! Horses of many different colors pulled them, and the horses looked like they were made out of jewels, sparkling and glinting in the sun. The chariots didn't look like they were cheap either, all of them either gold or silver in color. Men and women in long, black robes cracked whips against the jewel-horses, urging them on with each loud snap of their whips' tip.

And then, something slightly less dazzling happened. About a hundred feet past the on-ramp, Terra's car dropped onto the pavement. She watched with supreme disappointment as her tires "deflated," the water she'd made them with flowing out and away from where it belonged, then splashing against the side of a chariot that was quickly passing her in the next lane.

The chariot that had been behind her backed up a little and moved to her side, but instead of rushing right on by and ignoring her, it stopped, and a man with a shaved head and rather large, shockingly orange eyes climbed down from his ride and walked over to her car.

"I see your chariot has stopped moving. Do you need a ride?"

Terra didn't know whether she could trust him, but did she really have a choice? No, she realized, she did not, and so she took her bag out of the backseat of the now-useless car and got out of it, Onyx following her.

"Thank you, whatever your name is."

He helped her climb up next to him, and she secured her bag over her shoulder, placing Onyx inside. "Sorry, kitty, but I think you're safest in here."

"*Fine.*" He didn't sound like he thought it was fine, but they both knew he didn't really have a choice, either, unless he liked the idea of being trampled to death or crushed under a chariot—or both.

"Hold on," the man said, and she barely had enough time to grab the chariot's front bar before the man snapped his whip against the ruby horse's back and they shot forward, the air rushing past Terra's ears and tossing her hair around as they moved forward.

It was surprisingly fun, traveling down this freeway in such a unique way, and Terra forgot her worries for a few minutes, just enjoying the feel of the wind and the view of the beautiful horses and chariots traveling in the lanes to their left and right.

"My name is Hephastae, and what is yours?" He turned his head and looked at her, and she gasped as his features began to change. He'd started out looking very masculine, but his face was becoming delicate as she watched, feminine, and soon Hephastae was no longer a man, but a woman instead. She also had a shaved head, and the same large, orange eyes, but Hephastae's lips were fuller, and she now had a smaller nose and, as Terra glanced down, breasts. Really nice ones, it looked like, but not as lovely as the ones she had waiting back at home.

"Ah, you have noticed me changing. We are all Homofemme, or Femmehomo, if you prefer. I do not care which you use, but you may prefer to have 'femme' come first, as you seem to qualify for that word."

"Actually, I'm more butch than femme," she joked. Hephastae looked confused. "Never mind. I'm Terra, and the cat in my satchel is Onyx. Nice to meet you. We're on a quest right now."

"A quest, you say? Ah, I know just where to take you, in that case. It is only a few miles from here. You must be looking for Zeus's goblet."

"How the hell do you know about his goblet?" Terra fought the strong urge to cross her arms over her chest.

"Each and every being is on a quest, young woman, and I can see yours floating behind your eyes and glowing in your heart. Yours is a quest of love, I am guessing."

"Yeah, it is. It really, really is." Terra sighed and started to relax again. "So, you can help me?"

"I cannot find your goblet for you, dear girl, but I can show you the right path. It's up to you to follow it to its end. And to yours perhaps, too."

Terra grew tense and cold as soon as she heard the Femmehomo say this. "What does that mean? My end? Am I going to die?"

"Oh, I have said too much. Maybe you are and maybe you aren't. I do not know. Really, I don't."

It looked to Terra like she most definitely *did* know, but she could tell she wouldn't get another word out of the charioteer. And soon Hephastae was no longer "her" but becoming "him" again, her nose growing, her breasts disappearing, and her lips turning thin once more. The last change was a cleft developing in Hephastae's chin, and then Terra noticed that they were pulling off of the freeway and traveling along a smaller road.

Well, if Hephastae wouldn't tell her anything else about her possibly impending doom, she wouldn't speak again, either. She rode next to him in angry silence, only glancing in his direction when he changed and shrank back into a female once more.

"We're here," she said to Terra, and the horse slowed and came to a stop.

She got down from the chariot and helped Onyx out of her bag. He shook his head back and forth and stretched, first forward and then backward. "Oh, my, does it ever feel good to be out of that horrible, horrible bag. Remind me to never travel by chariot again."

"Hey, at least you aren't possibly headed straight toward death, little guy."

"Oh." Apparently Onyx hadn't heard Hephastae when she had said this.

"I guess I should thank you, despite your refusal to fill me in on certain…pertinent matters. Like whether I'm going to die or not." Now Terra did cross her arms, and Onyx huffed indignantly at her feet.

"He didn't fill you in?" Onyx looked up at Hephastae then, who was now seemingly a man.

"Never mind, Onyx, let's just get going. Thanks, Hephastae, I suppose."

"You are welcome, young woman, and I do indeed wish you luck. I always wish the pure of heart luck when I come across them."

"'Pure of heart?'" Terra mumbled as she walked away from Hephastae, Onyx at her side. "Yeah, freaking right. Hephastae obviously hasn't seen what I've been up to with Athene these last few days."

"Neither have I, thank all that's holy."

Terra grinned when he said this. She may have been walking straight toward death, but she was going to do it with good posture, so she straightened her back and kept the smile on her face as she started down the cliff and in the direction of whatever might happen to be awaiting her at its bottom.

❖

Eros had just arrived at the castle when he felt his father calling out to him. "Of *all* the times to bother me, just when I'm about to finish the quest," he muttered to himself. But his father was always to be obeyed, as he had always possessed more power than Eros—much, much more.

"Yes, Father?" He shut his eyes and held out his hand, muttering a phrase, and when he opened his eyes once more, an image of his father, a muscular, bald man in his late fifties, appeared right above his hand.

"Have you almost completed the quest?" No hello, no how are you doing…Not that Eros minded, really, after all of these years. All his father cared about was power and money…no, not about his one and only son—a son who happened to now be well on his way to acquiring much, much more of his father's two favorite things.

Eros fought his urge to scowl, then answered, frowning slightly despite himself. "Yes, Father, I'm almost finished. I'm at the castle where I've learned the goblet is housed, and it's only a matter of time before it's in my hands and the Werths' power is in yours." He left out the fact that in order to finish the quest, he'd have to kill the wizard who had the power of water, the wizard who had read as female when he'd tried to kill him, and when he'd appeared before him in the desert as Zeus. Things were always hazy when you were projecting yourself somewhere other than where your body lay. And in the woods, he had been too busy fighting the forest varmints to pay much attention to the attack he'd sent inside their home. He didn't even really know how such things worked, but after all this was taken care of, he wouldn't have to spend his weekly allowance on other Magic Ones' over-priced, magic trinkets.

His father's voice brought him out of his thoughts of vengeance. "Good, good. And the powers I've lent to you have been of some help?"

"Yes, your power of persuasion and your gift of fire have been incredibly helpful," he told his father. He really didn't like thanking him, but his father had trained him to do so over years of punishments, each one dealt out when he wasn't properly appreciative. "I couldn't have done it without them," he added, trying to keep all signs of sullenness out of his voice, but likely failing to do so.

"I am glad that you sound grateful. I will be quite relieved to have them back. And you have the other ring made by my witch jeweler? The one that will steal the power from the Werths' entire line? The power, and the life?" he added with a cold smile. "Oh, that Cer, she will be sorry she ever chose Zeus over me."

"What do you mean, Father?" Eros asked. This was something he had never heard before. Had his father courted Cer Werth in the past?

"Silence, you idiot!" The smile quickly left his father's face, replaced by the look Eros had learned to fear at a very young age—the look that said he had screwed up and disappointed his father, and he would pay for his mistake very, very soon. He felt a lick of his father's power, the painful heat that came with his fire—and with his anger.

"I'm sorry. I'm sorry, Father. Really, I am. I should go, though. Two of the competitors have been close behind me all along, and so I have to hurry. I can sense someone who is almost to the castle, not too far behind me. But they'll have to get past the next of the giants first. As though anyone could do *that* very easily without the help of your ring."

"Get on with it then, boy! Don't let someone else win. We must best everyone!" With that, his father snapped out of view.

"'We,' Father? Really?" He'd barely had to lift a hand, Eros thought as he used magic to open the castle's large wood doors. *I'm the one who had to scare the competition off.*

Why on earth someone was still following him, he didn't know. Nor did he know why, when he'd tried to kill Saturn, he had failed, or, even more surprisingly, why Saturn almost seemed more woman than man when he'd attacked him two nights before. It was also inexplicable that Saturn suddenly possessed what seemed to be a fountain of power. He could feel it touching his back as he entered the castle, like a fine, cool mist, a sensation that urged him on, toward the goblet, and toward the power that would soon be his and his alone. Once he had the Werths' power, once they had all dissolved into dust and left him with all their magic, there was no goddamn way in hell he'd share the power with his father.

That was the reason he'd come on this quest. That was what had kept him going throughout all of these trials. That was what pushed him through the palace's doors and onto the final part of the quest. Just vengeance. Revenge. Hatred.

Certainly not love.

Chapter Twenty-two

When Terra reached the bottom of the cliff, she felt a strong pull—a pull she was hesitant to follow. It was a pull she didn't especially like, because the slight tug against her skin was joined with a feeling of threat, threat that felt hot and intense and...and like cool rock, too?

Maybe they're separate things, she thought, as she rounded the corner of a huge boulder, ducking between it and another of equal size. And then a loud rumbling came from all around her. She watched, eyes wide open and mouth agape, as the rocks slowly began to move. It turned out they weren't rocks, not exactly, but a creature made out of stone—a fucking *giant* creature.

She turned to Onyx and, in a quiet voice, ordered him to run and hide. He dashed back the way they had come. At least he would survive this next threat, even if she didn't. She turned back to face the giant and began to assess her potential foe—and her potential doom, if he wasn't a friendly giant. Based on his facial expression, he didn't really look like one.

The giant had masculine features, and his face almost looked like it had been carved into the stone by a skilled artisan, because he was absolutely beautiful. But beautiful features aside, he also must have been at least thirty feet tall. A deep, menacing growl from him quickly distracted Terra from his gorgeous face. Besides, she wasn't a rockosexual, nor was she into giant men.

"My brother is dead. My brother Orthus is dead, woman! Are you here to kill me as well? You must be!" His voice sounded like rocks rubbing together, or perhaps large stones tumbling against one another. It was a lovely, soothing sound, but his words were terrifying, not soothing in the least. How on earth was she supposed to get past this gigantic monster?

And then she remembered the dagger, the one she'd killed the Wolfran with. If it could kill a Wolfran, perhaps it had a chance against this creature, too. She closed her eyes (a large risk around a beast like this creature, admittedly) and stretched out her hand. She thought of the coolness of metal and wrapped her hand around the dagger's handle in her mind. When she opened her eyes, there it was, floating in front of her hand. She wrapped her fingers around the real handle as tight as she could and placed her other hand over the one already gripping the dagger.

She felt herself drifting up off the ground now. Was the dagger doing that, or was she? Soon she was as high as the giant's waist, and then she ducked, shooting back down a few feet, so quickly her stomach lurched a little. The giant had pulled back one of his humongous hands and swung it straight at her. Instead of connecting with her body and smacking the life right out of her, it slammed into the cliff behind her. Flecks of stone and dirt flew in her direction, and again, she shot away from them, only a few dirt clods hitting her back and legs.

"I don't want to hurt you," she told him, "I just want to get past you!"

But the giant shouted, "Lies! Just like the beast before you, with the flaming horns, all lies! You witches and monsters all just want to kill me and my brothers!" His other fist flew at her, and again, she moved up a few feet, his punch missing her by a sizeable amount, this time just connecting with air.

The dagger moved back then, the dagger with a mind of its own, and her legs flew out in front of her, and before she could complete her next thought, Terra's feet slammed into the giant's upper chest and knocked him back a few feet.

"No!" he shouted, but he was falling, falling fast, and with a very loud crash, he had completely lost his footing, and he landed—hard—on his back. Terra flew down then, and the dagger swung down, too, coming to rest a hair's breadth away from his neck.

"Let me say it again—I don't want to hurt you. I just want to get past you, Giant. I am sorry your brother was killed, I really am." And then a thought entered Terra's head—possibly a very good one. She held up her left hand, stopping herself right before she raised her middle finger. It might have been the one with the ring on it, but she didn't want to risk making the giant any angrier than he already was. "I have something that might be able to help you. This ring is supposed to be able to bring people back to life. I don't know if it'll work on him, but it's worth a try, right?"

"I suppose so. Please let me get up, and I will lead you to him."

This time she moved through the air with her own intent, and she lowered the dagger, staring down at it. "Go on, you. Go back to wherever you belong." The dagger began to fade, and then it was gone. Now she was defenseless against this still very scary creature. Had she made the right decision?

"Follow me." He rose from the ground, and Terra backed up from him as he stood up, finally able to concentrate on the joy that came from flying. Then, still in the air, she followed the giant to a large opening in the cliff—a cave with one of the biggest mouths she'd ever seen. "He's in here, what's left of him."

"What's your name?" she asked as they entered the cave.

"Baryus. But you can call me Bar, if you manage to bring Orthus back to life. After all, if you succeed, you will forever be my friend."

"I hope we can be friends, then."

They continued into the cave, through a huge tunnel high and wide enough to accommodate a creature of Baryus's size. Then they came to a huge room, where a rock giant slightly smaller than Baryus lay. Two other giants sat beside him, and dark pebbles were slowly sliding down their cheeks. Were those tears?

"Okay," she said, landing softly on the deceased giant's chest. "Let's see if this works."

She laid her hands on his chest and visualized him coming back to life, but nothing was happening. How was she supposed to make the ring work? But then the ring grew warm, and her body began to grow colder just as quickly as the ring's heat grew. Her own temperature continued to fall, until she was shivering a little, the cold spreading throughout her body. Soon, she was so cold she was shaking, her breath coming out heavy and cool. She opened her eyes and watched as small puffs of sparking red clouds flowed from her mouth and onto the giant's chest.

His body heaved beneath her—once, twice—and then the heat returned to her body all at once. She turned her head and looked at Orthus's chest as it had begun to rise and fall, and the sound of the giant gasping for air came from slightly beyond where Terra stood.

"Am I...am I alive once more?" he said, his voice heaving along with his chest.

Terra rose up into the air again, flying a ways to his left and landing with a small *thud* on the ground near his shoulders. The two seated giants rose to their feet and walked over to their revived brother. Both shared looks of relief and were soon smiling—smiles that were gentle and slightly cautious—as they helped him into an upright position.

"It worked! It worked!" Baryus's wide grin held not even a glimmer of caution as he knelt, kissing his brother on each cheek as dozens of dark pebbles flowed down his face and hit his brother, each small rock coming with a quiet *thunk*ing sound as it made contact.

"It did, didn't it?" Terra looked down at the ring, but it was black now, instead of silver, and when she flexed her middle finger, it broke into tiny, ash-like pieces and floated to the cave's floor. "Well, guess I won't be saving any more lives with that, then."

"You may pass, young witch," Baryus told her now, "and if you ever need anything, call out my name, and I will be there as fast as an avalanche can tumble down a mountain."

Terra guessed that he couldn't *really* move that fast, but she still appreciated the offer, so she thanked him. She found herself feeling a little teary as she watched the three brothers helping Orthus slowly rise to his feet.

"You may call me Bar, by the way, friend." Baryus reached down and patted her on the head. Surprisingly, it was a gentle enough pat that she knew it wouldn't result in a concussion, or even a slight headache.

"Thanks, Bar. I have to get going, now, though. I have a goblet to find and a girl to marry."

"Watch out for the horned man," one of the brothers said. "He—"

"Yeah, yeah, I know. Everyone seems to be telling me that. I promise I will," she told the giants, and then she turned away from them and toward the cave's exit.

Onyx was waiting at the cave's entrance, and he ran up to her and placed his paws on her knees. "Terra, I was so worried about you! I didn't know...I didn't know if you were going to make it!" He was crying, his little face wet with tears, and Terra scooped him up into her arms and hugged him tight.

"I'm fine, kitty. But I think you should head back with me to your home. I don't know if it's going to be safe when I get to where I'm going." *Where the horned man probably is...where he's waiting for me.*

"Are you...are you sure?" Onyx sounded relieved, and although that made her a little sad, she couldn't blame him. If she failed to match this evil creature's power, if she failed to win, Onyx wouldn't stand a chance.

"I have a feeling there will be some doors ahead of us. I'm going to use the doorway stone again and send you back to my room. You'll be safe there, and I need to say hello to Athene in private." Hello, and, possibly, good-bye, she thought. But she didn't want to say it out loud. She was worried enough as it was, and she really didn't want to add a possible jinx to her chance of surviving this next trial. After all, Hephastae had mentioned the possibility of death, and there had also been her vision from the wine. But she didn't have a choice.

She turned to the left as she walked out of the cave and headed forward in the direction of the magical pull she was feeling, in the direction of the goblet. And, possibly, in the direction of her death.

It took her about a twenty-minute flight (after all, why walk when you can fly?) to reach the place where she was sure the goblet was located. This must have been where the heat she'd felt had been coming from, too, because the temperature made her feel as if it were a hot, dry day in the desert as a tall, menacing-looking castle came into view. The sky was dark above her, and she wouldn't regret leaving this place for a few blessed minutes. In terms of regrets about having to return here, though...

In that moment, she was desperate to hold Athene in her arms, and perhaps to also make love to her once more. Before she found the goblet. Before she met up with the horned man. Before...before she died?

Chapter Twenty-three

Terra placed the doorway stone in front of the castle's large doors and placed Onyx beside it. Then she grabbed the handles of the doors and pulled them open, her feet off the ground as she opened a doorway to her room back at the castle. Once Onyx was inside, and after one last hug with him, she shut the doors and then opened them again, this time walking through them and into Athene's room, where she lay sleeping in her bed.

Trying her best to be light on her feet, she walked up to Athene—her first love…the love of her life—and watched her sleep for a few moments. Athene was lying on her side, her hands nestled against her head and her beautiful hair flowing out behind her on the pillow, a river of lustrous gold that came close to glowing in the moonlight. It was almost a shame to wake her, to move this perfect vision who lay underneath the covers in front of her, but Terra was still very aware that she might never speak to her again. So wake her she did, reaching forward and brushing a few strands of hair off Athene's face.

"What?" Athene's voice was thick and sleepy, but she seemed to wake right up as soon as she saw it was Terra who had woken her. "Terra! You're here!" She grinned, her eyes still a little more shut than usual, but her voice sounded fully awake and full of life.

"You sure came to quickly." Terra gave an uneven smile, one side of her mouth going all the way up as Athene shot up and enveloped her in an incredibly tight hug. She'd thought for a while that you could sense how in love with you someone was by the way they touched you, and she could always feel immense love in every touch of Athene's hands, be it a passionate one or something more subtle, like when Athene held her hand while they watched a movie on her bedroom TV.

"Long time no see, huh?" Terra joked.

"It feels like it's been a lot longer than it actually has," Athene told her. "Waiting here without a clue of what you're up to—I get scared, you know. I'm pretty sure you haven't been coming up against anything very dangerous, but still, I can't help worrying just a bit." She pulled back from Terra then, and bit her lip. It wasn't the sexual variety of a lip-bite—it was the nervous type. Terra had always loved that she did it at both times—when she was immensely turned on or when she was nervous.

She cupped Athene's chin and kissed her, hard. The kiss spoke of their many months together. It was a kiss that spoke of her love for this woman, this person...her love for Athene. She pulled back after a few long minutes, and now it was her turn to look concerned. "I have to tell you something, Athene. Something really bad, something you won't like." She told her about Hephastae, about the horned man, and finally, Terra forced herself to tell her that this might be the last time they saw each other.

Athene was crying by the time she had finished sharing this information, but instead of saying anything, she put her lips back on Terra's. As they kissed, she slowly and gently stripped Terra of her clothes. Athene had been sleeping naked, so as each piece of Terra's clothing was removed, she was also treated to a view of Athene's beautiful, absolutely perfect body, her skin pale and gorgeous in the moonlight. It was a lovely contrast against Terra's darker skin, the rich, deep brown of hers complementing Athene's pale, porcelain arms, thighs, and torso.

Each of these completely perfect parts of her lover's body was now pressed up against her own arms, thighs, and torso, Athene's body wrapped around hers in a tight, lover's embrace. But hopefully not a lover's parting, Terra thought with more than a touch of desperation. Hopefully this would not be the last time their bodies would be locked together like this.

Terra tried not to think about this possibility as they kissed, though, and she almost succeeded, as Athene found her wet cunt with her right hand and began to thrust her fingers inside her hole. This time, they didn't need magic—no flowing silk, no flowing ink, just flowing fingers, flowing in and out of Terra and then in and out of Athene, as Terra's fingers found Athene's opening as wet and as ready as her own…if not more. They both reached deeper inside each other, Terra first, and then Athene following suit. Then they were both curling their fingers forward, finding their partner's delicious, raised spot deep inside their cunt, and each woman massaged the other's with her fingers as they kissed and wrapped themselves around one another.

Terra couldn't help thinking, then, that it wouldn't be such a bad thing if this moment were to never end…if she could just keep fucking her lover, thrusting her fingers in and out of her, thrusting her body against Athene's forever. She didn't want to leave her, didn't want to go back to the castle, and she didn't want the pleasure of being touched in such an intense, passionate, loving way to go away, not even for a moment. She knew Athene was thinking the same thing from the way she clung to her—desperately—and from the way her fingers seemed hungrier than ever before—hungry for her to come, for her to gush all over Athene's palm and thighs.

But it had to end, despite what either of them wanted so desperately, and soon Athene was making small noises against Terra's lips, small moans and pants, sounds that grew louder and louder until she came, screaming, against Terra's mouth. No bubble popped up then, no bubble to block their sounds, and she and Terra called out into the night as they both came so, so hard. Their passion had thoroughly soaked the sheet beneath them, soaked into the mattress, and had also splashed against their thighs and legs and hands and arms...

And then, Athene's bedroom door slammed open, and Cer stood there, her face first full of shock, and then full of fury. "*What* is going on? Athene, what are you doing with her?"

Before she could give it a second thought, Terra jumped out of bed and grabbed her clothes. She shut her eyes tight and heard Cer rushing toward her, heard Athene begin to try to explain, and thought to herself, please, please, please work!

Then she couldn't hear Cer anymore, or Athene, either, and so she risked opening her eyes.

She was back in front of the castle, wearing her clothes again. No doorway stone had been needed this time, it seemed. Her powers had grown yet again, and she hoped they had grown enough to help her find the goblet; to help her kick the horned man's ass; and to help her get back home, then try to explain it all to Cer in a way she would understand. She didn't think she had a chance in hell of accomplishing that last part, based on the look on Cer's face as she had rushed into her daughter's room. But perhaps Cer loved Athene enough to want her to be truly happy...which would mean wanting her to be with Terra.

But she needed to put on her battle-face now. So she squared her shoulders and kicked the doorway stone away from the door. Then, using her powers, she slammed open the two heavy castle doors and started inside. She was either going to her doom or to be with Athene forever, and it didn't take a genius to figure out which she was hoping for as she stepped into the castle and shut the doors behind her with a swift wave of her hands.

It was dark inside, but not so dark that she couldn't make everything out well enough. The place was stuffed full of what looked like close-to-priceless treasures. She'd known Zeus and Cer were well off, but if this place was theirs, they were much, much more than merely "rich."

The large hall—or entryway—had an incredibly high ceiling, almost impossibly high. Beautiful curves were carved into the walls on either side of Terra, their dips and valleys filled with large opals and other semi-precious stones. Chandeliers hung from the ceiling with dozens of lit candles in each of them, and tapestries were hanging along each wall. Terra looked at each of the ornate weavings as she walked forward. They all showed witches and wizards using magic to cure people of illnesses, to stop humans from fighting one another, and a number of other honorable acts. Terra was saddened as she realized this must have been what the Magic Ones used to be like, in the distant past, before things changed and they became lazy, greedy, and uncaring. Maybe, if she made it through this test, and Cer and Zeus accepted her into their family (yeah, right), she could do a thing or two with her new abilities to help the world, instead of only helping herself get what she wanted…and, she thought, needed. In other words, Athene.

But was she going to make it through this final trial? She'd know soon enough, that much was certain, because the whole palace was filled with heat. The temperature in the entry-hall was causing little beads of sweat to form on her forehead as she continued walking down the hall's length with surprisingly steady steps. She might have been scared, but this was her only hope of being with Athene. And if she reached the goblet first, she'd be saving Athene from a life with that asshole Eros.

Those two thoughts filled her with more bravery than she'd previously thought she had. But as she left the hall and began to hear small, creepy scurrying noises, some of that bravery flew away and left her with a touch of fear in its place. Where were those noises coming from? More important, were they going to be a threat?

As she tensed her arms at her sides, her left hand brushed against something small and cylindrical sticking out of her pocket. She placed her hand around it and pulled it out: it was the spyglass Sun and Moon had given to her. Lifting it to her right eye, she closed the other and stared through it, stifling a cry of fear as she finally saw what was making the noises.

Foot-high, skeletal creatures were inching forward, heading straight at her. Smoke drifted off them, because they were all covered in flames. Much worse than that was the fact that they were closing in on her. Low growls were coming from each of their wide, scary mouths, and it seemed that the horrible creatures knew she had noticed them now, because they sped up their movement in her direction. Some of them dashed across the walls, some of them had bat-like wings and flew, and some simply ran on their little sharp-clawed feet.

Terra remembered her power over water then. But how could she put out the creatures' fires, if no water was nearby? So she shut her eyes—it was a risky move, but one that felt necessary—and raised her arms, one hand pointing left, the other to her right. The ground began to shake, but she didn't open her eyes. Either this would work or it wouldn't, and opening her eyes wouldn't change which side the coin of chance landed on.

Then she heard a low, rumbling sound, which turned into the sound of rushing water, and she finally opened her eyes when she heard a few high-pitched shrieks of pain. Beautiful, dark-blue water was flowing straight toward her, and it seemed to be accomplishing exactly what she had hoped it would. As it flowed forward, it splashed over the horrible little fire-creatures, and she smiled just a bit as she heard their cries of pain and distress. One after another, each of them was submerged in the water, and their flames sizzled out and they disappeared. She could see the remaining creatures without using the spyglass now; she could see each creature as it disappeared from the room as the water continued to rush forward.

It finally slowed when it reached her, and she leaned down, stroking it gently and thanking it in its own wet-sounding tongue. How she had learned to speak "water" she didn't know, but it seemed to delight at hearing its own language, caressing her fingers with small, cool kisses. She reveled in the feel of it flowing past her and around her lower legs. Its touch was gentle and lusciously soft as it brushed against her skin. And then it was gone, and the hall was empty, the floor even dry to the touch, she discovered, and so now it was time to continue. But instead of putting the spyglass back in her pocket, she raised it to her eye again, because she remembered what Moon had told her: that it would help her find things that did not wish to be found. Things like evil fire-creatures, of course, and—possibly, hopefully—things like missing goblets.

Chapter Twenty-four

The pull she'd felt, the one that had led her to the castle, seemed to have vanished by the time the water was gone, because hell if she knew what direction to go in next. "Fuck," she said softly, and her voice echoed in the high-ceilinged room. *Shit!* If the horned man hadn't sensed her coming—which he probably had, given the evil little fire-shitheads—he'd certainly heard that loud noise!

Well, onward was her only option at this point, so onward she went. The huge room she was now entering was just as beautiful as the hall had been. Scattered around the room were at least twenty tall, straight-backed, black-lacquered chairs with velvet, tasseled cushions on each of their seats. The chairs were placed around huge oval tables, made of dark wood with beautiful turquoise- and ruby-colored inlay around their rims. She let her fingers brush against one of them as she walked past it and felt the pleasurable vibration of magic singing against her skin. As she lifted her hand, the table shook slightly and rose toward her hand, almost as if it didn't want to part with her.

"Stay, Mr. Table, stay," she said with a grin.

Terra heard a *harrumph*, then, and practically jumped out of her skin. "It's *Missus* table, little lady. *Mister* Table is to my left."

"Sorry, Missus Table." Terra stifled a laugh. This was her first conversation with a piece of furniture, after all, and definitely her first conversation with tetchy furniture! "I apologize for not getting your gender right."

"Ah, well, I suppose you couldn't tell, being a witch and all. It's nice to have someone new around, though, I must say. Especially someone who didn't threaten to burn me to ashes if I didn't tell him where the goblet was. Not that he was able to, mind you. We're protected from destruction, just like the goblet is."

"Can you help *me* find it, then?" Terra looked down at the female table and waited.

"Hmm. You may have just soaked me with water, which I did *not* appreciate, but those little beastly things that were headed straight at me probably would have made me even *more* uncomfortable. So…I suppose I owe you a debt, Witch, and that debt I will pay you. Put that spyglass on top of me, and I'll pass some of my knowledge of the castle into it."

Terra did as Missus Table asked, gently placing the spyglass on her surface. The spyglass wobbled briefly as soon as she let go, but when she reached back down to steady it, the table spoke again, saying, "Don't touch it, or it won't work!" in a very grouchy tone.

"Sorry!" Terra told her.

"All right, Witch," the table said a few moments later, and Terra watched as the spyglass floated up a few feet and stopped right next to her eye. "I'm done. Just follow its path, and look through it when it stops. I'd watch out for that horrible horned fire-bastard if I were you, though. He's not the *nicest* person I've ever met, that's for darn sure!"

"So everyone keeps telling me," she told Missus Table.

The spyglass began to float forward then, and Terra followed it. She had to walk quickly, as it seemed the spell didn't care in the least that a human could only move so fast. Soon enough, she had to break into a run, following the spyglass along a twisting path from room to room until she almost ran into it when it stopped, suddenly, in front of a small, nondescript door.

"Spyglass marks the spot, I guess," she said to herself. Hopefully it was only to herself, because she knew—between her echoing voice in the room full of tables and the pounding sound of her feet across the castle's floors—that the horned man with the power of fire couldn't be too far behind.

Terra tested the doorknob, and what do you know, it wasn't locked. She felt it turning to the right in her hand from almost no pressure at all. Terra eased the door open, a not-nearly-quiet-enough creak coming from it as it swung open into the small room beyond it. The room held a desk, behind which was a large, square window. Moonlight streamed through the window, painting the whole room in shimmery silver.

Terra plucked the spyglass out of the air and placed it in front of her eye as she stood in the doorway, and there it was— Zeus's goblet—sitting on the table. It was the color of the light filling the room and looked like it was made of mist, its edges blurred and its body almost transparent.

"Eureka!" Terra shouted happily, and then she shrieked as she felt a burning-hot hand grab her by the neck and lift her up off the ground, flinging her at least ten feet down the hallway and away from the room.

As she passed through the hallway at a nauseating speed, she heard a loud sizzling sound and then realized she was levitating, seemingly from her own powers. But the sizzling sound wasn't coming from her. It came instead from a figure across the hallway from her—the horned man.

Roiling flames leapt from each of his horns, and though he held a ball of crackling fire in each hand, his face was still hidden in darkness. But once he reached the doorway of the room containing the goblet, his face was lit up by the moonlight, and Terra whispered his name. "Eros." Her voice shook a little as she said this, but she used some of her magic to lift herself up into a fully upright position, her feet hovering a little above the floor. Terra watched, then, full of fear, as the horned man—or Eros—entered the goblet's room, leaving only moments later. His hands still held the fireballs, the goblet neither in his right hand nor his left.

"Where is it, you bitch?" he growled, the rumble of his low voice reaching Terra and almost shoving her to the floor. But she managed to stay afloat and just smiled at him.

"You can't see it, can you?" She didn't try to hide the haughtiness in her voice, instead letting it leap right out of her lips, along with a touch of pride. *She* had found the goblet, and *she* had completed the entire quest, and this monster, standing before her, had *not*. "You can't see it," she repeated, this time with more certainty.

But that seemed to be the wrong thing to say. Eros yelled out with fury and then hurled one of his fireballs right at her. Terra shot to the right, the fireball barely missing her, almost touching her skin as it flew past and hit the wall. The wall began to burn, the fire quickly spreading in Terra's direction.

The next fireball Eros threw didn't miss. It hit her squarely in the chest, her body becoming enveloped in flames quicker than her eyes could track. She screamed as they burned against her skin. It was the most painful thing she'd ever felt. She tried to fight her way out of the fire, but it was no use. Eros had won, and though she still continued to struggle as he raised his hand, she couldn't stop him from drawing her forward, closer and closer, until his face—his angry, dastardly, cheating face—was inches from hers.

"You will get me the goblet, or you will die. You choose which it will be."

"What, I don't get a third option?" She might have been in immense pain, but she still had a little more fight left in her. This was all about Athene, after all, and she couldn't lose, not when something so precious was at stake.

"Of course you don't. Can't you see that I am holding your life in my hands, Witch? Can't you see that I could put out your own flame of life in a mere instant?" He smiled with dark, angry eyes, and the fire got hotter. Terra could barely breathe, and while she loved Athene with all her heart, was giving this man her life going to help anything? She had to fight this—she had to win...but how?

Her answer came in a cold, incredibly pissed-off voice right behind her. "Put out that fire, Eros, and let my daughter's lover go."

Even despite the horrible pain of Eros's fire, Terra could still feel the power behind her. It burned stronger than the fire, but this was a cold, chilling burn, one that slowly, bit by bit, lowered the temperature of the heat surrounding Terra's body.

"Cer? What are you doing here? And what do you mean, your daughter's lover?" Eros looked truly shocked, and Terra found a bit of hope returning as Cer's face came into view on her left. Her body was glowing, brighter than the moonlight, brighter than the burning light coming from Eros's flames and the fire that still surrounded Terra.

"Put out these flames, or I will make sure you are very, very, *very* sorry, young man."

"Cer...please...I...I am..." He looked terrified, and it seemed he was well aware that he was no match for Cer.

But then he smiled in a most horrible way and raised his hand and shot a spray of flames from his fingers, the fire surrounding Terra now burning even hotter than before. "I'll take her with me, then!" he shouted, and the heat around her rose and rose, sucking the breath out of her...sucking the life out of her.

I'm sorry, Athene. I failed you. Terra's thoughts began to grow foggy, and although the fire around her burned incredibly brightly, everything was still growing dark.

Terra thought she heard someone say, "No, Eros, no, you won't!" And then the coldest sensation she'd felt in her life spread across her skin, spread into her as well, and she began to shake, violently, from the freezing feeling that rushed throughout her entire body. She began to cough as she shook, and she slowly drifted to the ground. The fire was out, and she was alive, and slowly, reality came back to her.

She saw the hallway again, saw Cer and Eros shooting fire and ice at each other, sometimes striking each other and sometimes missing. Then she watched as Eros yelled, "Father, help me!" and Terra looked on as his whole body turned to flames, every inch of him fire, every inch except for a ring on his left thumb. Right after she noticed the ring, he slammed Cer against the wall, pinning her to it, and it looked as though he just might win after all.

But that was *completely* unacceptable. So Terra pushed herself up off the floor, shut her eyes, and thought of water. She thought of every single drop of water she'd seen in her life. The water running into the sink in her bathroom. The small river and the koi pond near the mansion. The ocean she'd visited with her father and mother every summer until her mother died and she and her father moved into the Werths' mansion. She even pictured the fluid that had soaked the sheets when she and Athene had last had sex, and then she thought of Athene, her lovely, loving face and the beautiful smile on it whenever she looked at Terra.

Terra's eyes shot open, and she flew off of the floor, and she raised her hands. She heard a sound like the ocean on a stormy day, waves crashing violently against each other, each of them hungry for rain; she heard the rushing sound of a river...the rushing sound of hundreds of rivers; she heard Athene's juices splashing against the bed and her thighs. And then the whole hallway—and she just knew, somehow, the whole *castle*—filled with water.

She was floating, now, surrounded by water, but somehow, she could still breathe. She began to paddle in Eros and Cer's direction, and Cer was breathing, too, but Eros was not. He was choking on the water, clutching at his chest and neck, and his eyes seemed to plead with Terra as she looked into them. She knew her own were completely empty of compassion for him as he began to drown.

But what would Athene have done in this situation? And what would her mother have wanted her to do? After a moment's thought, she swam up to him, putting her mouth to his, and gave him a few mouthfuls of air as she removed the ring he wore, the one she was certain gave him the power he'd had up until that moment. The power that had almost killed her, the power she now felt flowing into her body as she crushed the ring in her hand, turning it to little flecks of gold that floated away down the water-filled hallway. She looked at Cer then. They made eye contact, and Athene's mother swam a few feet forward and took Terra's hand, bringing it to her mouth and kissing it softly.

"Athene told me everything," she said to Terra. "And while you may not believe it, I do want the best for her, and you seem to be exactly what she needs...and deserves. Now, my dear, how about we get that goblet and head home?"

What could Terra do but smile and nod? So she did each, and they swam into the small room, Terra first, and she picked up the goblet. She didn't need to use the spyglass to see it any longer, nor was she unable to pick it up, despite the fact that it looked like her hand would go right through it. The goblet solidified as she took it off the table, and she heard a loud, shrill ringing sound, which grew louder and louder until she feared it would shake her apart, and then she realized it was coming from the goblet.

"Time to leave!" Cer shouted over the incredibly loud ringing, and she took Terra's hand in hers. Terra gripped the goblet tight in her other hand. No fucking *way* she was going to let go of it now.

Chapter Twenty-five

With a loud splash, Terra and Cer landed on the floor of the castle's dining hall. Both of them were soaking wet, and for a few moments, the shock of the sudden change of scenery kept Terra from taking in her surroundings. She just lay on the floor with her eyes shut and luxuriated in the exquisite pleasure of having won the quest. She was grinning, and she'd never been so completely happy in her entire life.

But her joy quickly doubled as she felt arms wrapping around her, instantly recognizing the familiar scent of Athene's favorite shampoo as it wafted in her direction. Athene put her lips to Terra's ear and said, "I'm never letting you go again, Terra. And I'm definitely not letting you out of my sight any time soon, either."

Terra wrapped her exhausted arms around her, smiling even wider. "Sounds good to me. Especially if there's a bed and some nudity involved."

She heard a few sounds of laughter at her words, and then she *did* take in the room, as it seemed that she, Cer, and Athene weren't alone. With a large amount of struggling and some leaning on Athene for support, she got to her feet.

They weren't even close to alone, she now saw. No, they were practically surrounded, all of the mansion's staff and residents scattered around the room. Her father and Zeus were standing next to each other, with matching looks of shock on their faces. Then both of them rushed forward, her father hugging her tight. "I missed you, sweetheart! I'm so, so glad you made it back! And you succeeded!" Her father's voice matched his words, filled with equal parts awe and affection. When her father let go of her, Zeus approached her next and held out his hand.

"I believe some thanks are in order," he said to her, his voice sounding a fair bit less empty of doubt than it usually did. "My wife lent me her seeing mirror, and we all watched the battle. I tried to travel there to help, but the doorway stone Cer used to get there didn't work. I was terrified, to be honest, to be completely unable to help my dear wife when Eros had her pinned to the wall. I owe you an immense debt of gratitude." Terra was surprised to see that he was crying, and then he pulled her to his chest, wrapping her in a tight hug as he began to shake and cry even harder.

"In terms of that debt of gratitude, what would you say to paying me with your daughter's hand in marriage?" Terra patted him on the back, feeling a little uncomfortable hugging him and a fair bit more uncomfortable with his tears.

"Gladly!" he sobbed, and instead of letting her go, he squeezed her harder.

"Uh, Zeus, you're kind of crushing me."

He quickly released her at those words, backing up a few feet. "Excuse me, Terra. It's not every day that you almost lose your wife." He wiped his cheeks with his hands and cleared his throat. "I believe a banquet of celebration is in order."

The banquet occurred that very night. Since Freo knew all of Terra's favorite dishes, that was what they had, dining on salads filled with goat cheese and candied walnuts, Cornish game hen with rosemary and lemon and garlic mashed potatoes, a cheese course, and crème brulèe for dessert. It couldn't have possibly tasted better to Terra, but later that evening, when she climbed into bed with Athene without having to sneak into her room, she decided that Athene's mouth tasted even more wonderful than the whole meal put together.

"You taste amazing," she told Athene, in between kisses.

"Vanilla lip gloss," her soon-to-be wife told her the next time she came up for air.

"No, it's not that, it's you. You taste like the woman I love. That's a taste I'll never, ever get tired of. Not as long as I live."

"Let's hope so, because we're getting married in just a few weeks."

"Why don't we consummate our wedding a little early?" Terra suggested, as she slid her hand in between Athene's thighs.

"You mean like we've been doing for months? Hmm," Athene said, cupping Terra's breast and moving her mouth much closer to its erect nipple. "Give me a minute or two to think it over. I'll tell you my decision in just a bit."

As Athene kissed her nipple, Terra sighed and relaxed even further against the bed's multiple pillows. This was their first time making love since she'd returned, and her first time being able to spend the entire night in Athene's room. Although it wasn't the first time Athene had taken her nipple into her mouth, Terra couldn't help but think that it didn't feel any less amazing than it had that first night they'd slept together. No, not one single *bit* less amazing.

"Mmm, you're doing that just right." As she said this, Athene slipped her hand in between her thighs, a hand that began to vibrate as it played with her clit. "A new trick, huh?" She spread her lips into a wide smile as Athene's vibrating hand buzzed away against her cunt, and then her lips began to part more and more as she gasped and sighed and moaned, getting closer and closer to the precarious spot between not having come yet and falling into a delicious orgasm. And then she tumbled over the edge, falling into bliss, bliss that seemed destined to occur at least four times before she said, "Enough, enough! Oh, God, Athene, you're so, so good. Just…just give me a moment, and then it'll be your turn."

"Take all the time you want," Athene said, placing her soft lips on Terra's mouth. "Now that you're officially mine, we have a fucking large amount of time."

"That's good." Terra sighed as their lips parted for a moment, and then she began to make out with Athene—her soon-to-be wife!—once more. "That's so, so good."

When she'd regained enough strength, she kissed and licked her way down Athene's body and then placed a vibrating tongue and vibrating lips onto Athene's pussy. Athene's back arched in an instant. "Oh, you naughty, naughty…girl…how do you *ever* catch on so fast?"

Their fun continued into the early morning hours, as they took turns making each other come, took turns placing fingers, and dildos, and whatever else struck their fancy, deep inside each other. But eventually they were both exhausted, and so, begrudgingly, Terra suggested they call it a night. Athene acquiesced and lay on her side. Terra spooned her and placed her hand gently on Athene's hip.

Then she began to sing to Athene, a song her mother had sung her to sleep with when she was little. It was a song about a prince and a princess, and how their love for one another spanned streams, rivers, and oceans, and Terra smiled as she sang, because now that love was hers. Just as Athene was now hers, and she was now Athene's. As she drifted off to sleep, she realized that for the first time in ages, she was excited about what the next morning might bring. After all, she had a wedding to prepare for and plan, a wedding and a whole life to spend with the lovely woman in her arms. She knew that some people got cold feet before these things, but her feet were practically on fire, getting ready to walk the aisle...or, perhaps, to stand at the altar. Either way, she would be there with Athene, and they would be joined together, woman and woman, wife and wife.

Her excitement made it hard for her to sleep, but finally she did. She didn't dream at first, but then she began to, and it was her mother whom she dreamed of.

❖

Terra was sitting on a porch swing, sipping some mint iced tea, slowly swinging back and forth as she looked out across the sunny garden in front of her. The house seemed familiar, and she tried to place it, but failed. And then she heard a voice, coming from her left, and she knew exactly where she was—she was at home, and the voice was her mother's, calling her in for dinner. She quickly finished the tea and raced inside, right into her mother's waiting arms.

"Nerit! Mom! I've...I've missed you so much!" Terra's cheeks quickly became wet with tears, and she squeezed Nerit tight as she cried.

"My dear, darling girl, it's wonderful to see you, too. We haven't much time, you and I, so let's make it count. I've prepared supper for us—pot roast and mashed potatoes, your favorite. And you can either have more mint tea or some wine, if you'd like. I make it myself, in the shed near the house. There are grapes growing nearby, and your other relatives help me make it—and help me drink it, too," she said with a warm laugh.

Terra pulled back and looked at her mother—her hair, her face, everything was the same. "Am I...am I really here with you? I mean, this isn't just a dream?"

"Yes, I have been granted the ability to give you passage into my world, where all of us Magic Ones go when we...when we die." Nerit brushed a few strands of Terra's hair behind her ear and kissed her on the forehead. "Now, why don't we eat? I'm looking forward to hearing about your life these days, more details about the little bits and pieces I've been able to see over the years I've been gone."

Terra made herself let go of her mom then, but doing so was a challenge—possibly just as big a challenge as the quest had been. She sat down at the table and proceeded to tell Nerit about all she had missed. "Well, you already know I've fallen madly, deeply in love with a woman—with Athene. And you also probably know my powers have been growing, and they're pretty damn awesome at this point in time." She scooped some mashed potatoes onto her plate and made them into a bowl for the pot roast, just like she had when she was little.

"I see that some things haven't changed at all, though," Nerit said with a gentle laugh.

Her mother's laugh—Goddess, Terra thought, how she had missed it...how she had missed everything about her mother. "So, I guess you don't know that Dad and I, we're living and working with the Werths, whom I'm pretty sure you've heard of. We both miss you, tons, but we're getting by, I suppose. He hasn't found anyone since you, well, you know." Terra took a bite of mashed potatoes and meat then, and it was just as delicious as it always had been, rich and sweet and so tender it practically melted on her tongue. "You were always such a good cook. The chef at the mansion is really good. Her name's Freo. She seems to like Dad, but he hasn't really noticed, I don't think."

"Either that or he won't allow himself to notice. I want you to tell him I'm fine with him moving on. It's certainly been long enough." Her mom smiled and placed her hand over Terra's. "I'm glad you've found love, my dear, but I hope your father can do the same someday, too. I'm curious, though—do you approve of Freo?"

"She's no 'you,' not at all, but she's very sweet, very kind to me, unlike the rest of the mansion's staff." Then Terra had a wicked thought. "I wonder if I'll be allowed to do some rearranging and cull a few members of the household's staff?" Terra smiled as she said this, despite the inherent—and obvious to her—evil of the idea. No, she'd turn the other cheek, although it wouldn't hurt to ask them to fetch things for her, and maybe start to ask her "how high?" as well. A few idle threats might be nice, too…

"I'd guess that a lot is bound to change now—for your father, for you, both with your abilities and your partnerships." Nerit raised her glass of tea and winked at Terra as she brought it to her lips.

"Partner*ships*? Do you know something I don't?"

"Perhaps I do. I was allowed to watch your father a few times while you were on your quest, and he seemed to spend a lot of his free time in the mansion's kitchen. With a pretty, short woman who was always cooking. It looked like they got along with each other quite well, Terra. Quite, quite well."

"That's great to hear. I was hoping he would eventually… you know, that he would notice her back."

"I believe he has. I also think you have brought the two of them together, by leaving for those few days." Nerit rose from the table then, and went over to the house's screen door. Terra watched her as she did, her beautiful mother lit up like a goddess by the early evening light.

Terra sighed at the sight. "You always were so beautiful, Mom."

"Thank you, honey. You're beautiful too, you know. Beautiful and so, so special. I'm glad Athene has noticed your specialness, and I hope she is able to bring you all the love I can't." Her mother's voice sounded thick and shaky, and when she turned her eyes were damp, tears beginning to slide down her cheeks. She walked over to Terra and leaned down slowly. "You have made me more proud than I can possibly put into words, Terra." Nerit placed her lips on her forehead and kissed her gently.

The room began to fade then, and Terra tried desperately to hold on to everything in it. But it was gone a few seconds later, and then she was waking up in Athene's bed with a nuzzle against her neck. "It's time to wake up, Terra. Let's greet the day with each other, and then I'll call downstairs and have breakfast delivered. Whatever you want to eat, it's yours. The same goes for any possible appetizers I can provide for you." Athene was smiling when she looked up at Terra's face, but she seemed to notice her mood in an instant. "What's wrong, sweetie?"

"I was with...I was with my mom tonight," Terra said in a far-off voice. "I went to where she is now, and we talked, and she held me, and..." and here Terra felt her throat grow tight and tense, "and she told me how proud she is of me, and how glad she is we've found each other."

"Oh, Terra!" Athene pulled her into a hug and smoothed down her hair. "It was...are you sure it was real? I mean, no, I'm sorry, what a stupid question. With the level of power you have now, you'd have known if it was or wasn't."

"Yes, yes, it was real. That's why, well, I think if it had just been a dream, it wouldn't have meant so much to me, you see. I've dreamed about her before, and while it always made me sad, it wasn't as special. Or as painful, either." Terra was surprised when the tears she'd been expecting didn't come. Instead, she found herself feeling stronger, growing less sad and more joyful as each moment passed—as each moment in her love's arms flowed by. "I think," she said, pulling back gently from Athene, "I'd like waffles. With whipped cream and fruit. And orange juice, and bacon. And coffee. With cream and sugar. And," she said, letting a wide grin spread across her face, "after breakfast, and perhaps after a quickie, I'd like to start planning our wedding. What do you think? Do you think I can have all of that? Am I asking for too much?"

"Only if you want the quickie to come after breakfast instead of before it. Then you'd *definitely* be asking for too much."

Terra laughed, and then she tackled Athene down against the bed, and they didn't use magic for a single second of their lovemaking. After all, who needs magic when you have someone to love, and that someone loves you back?

After the sex, and after eating far too much food, Terra insisted that they go right downstairs and start planning the wedding. "But first, first I need to ask my dad about something my mom told me last night."

"What is it? Tell me, please." Athene and Terra were getting dressed when she asked, as some of Terra's wardrobe had been ordered along with the breakfast. Terra had insisted that Isis bring both her clothes and the meal, and she had looked none too happy at serving Terra instead of the other way around.

"It's about Freo and my dad. My mom said something about them spending a lot of time together while I was gone. I'm hoping he finally got a clue and decided to start his life up again."

"She's definitely a good match for him—they'd be so cute together!" Athene made an annoyingly girlish squealing noise at the end of her sentence, but Terra decided she would forgive her for it, just this once, since it had to do with her dad finding love again.

Once they were both dressed, Athene said they should meet in the mansion's main living room, and she'd make sure someone came by with some fabric swatches and some patterns of possible dresses for her and suits for Terra. Terra remembered about her plans for the Hoomes then, and she brought their song to the front of her mind. But first, she had something more important to attend to.

When Terra asked one of the staff's cleaning ladies if her father was out at the stables, she replied that the last time she'd seen Zachary, he was headed toward the kitchen. Good, Terra thought as she made her way there, and she was smiling as she began to open the kitchen's door.

Inside the kitchen, Freo was standing behind the heavy wooden worktable, wearing an apron and covered in flour, and Zachary was standing to her left. Neither of them noticed Terra as she walked into the room. She noticed the smiles on each of their faces, though. And she also noticed the pink rose sitting on the table next to Freo's hand.

"So what should we do on it?" Freo was saying to her father.

"Do on what?" Terra asked.

Both of their heads whipped in her direction. Her dad started blushing a bit, and Freo smiled and looked down for a moment. "On our first date," she said when she looked back up. "That is, if you approve of your father going out with me. I wouldn't dream of doing it without his daughter's permission."

"I've been waiting—eagerly—for this to happen for ages. Of course I'm okay with it!" Terra ran up to her father and hugged him. "So is Mom," she whispered into his ear.

Her father looked even more surprised than he had when Terra had first entered the room. "She…is? You mean…?"

"I'll tell you all about it later. Right now, you have a first date to plan, and I have a wedding to plan, too." She kissed her dad on the cheek, then did the same to Freo.

"My!" Freo exclaimed. "Someone seems to be jolly today!"

"Must be all the love in the air." And with those words Terra left the room, the sounds of Freo and her dad resuming their date-planning following her out of the room.

From eleven that morning until four that afternoon, she learned that planning a wedding was a darn bit more complicated than planning a first date. She hoped her father and Freo weren't having a hard time figuring out their own plans, because she sure as hell was having trouble making hers and Athene's.

But one month later, their wedding day arrived. Despite a touch of jitters and worrying every few hours about everything going wrong, Terra was delighted when everything went right. Onyx was the first to walk down the aisle, carrying their two rings in a heather-gray silk pouch attached to his collar. He had been overjoyed when Terra had asked the Werths' magical acquaintances and found not one, but two gay cats who were now living with him. He'd told her that juggling two boyfriends was far too challenging, but he hadn't sounded all that unhappy about it.

Next down the aisle was Freo, dressed in a knee-length, green dress covered with delicate, pink flowers. She looked almost as happy as Terra felt. Maybe...or, perhaps, obviously, it was all the time she'd been spending with Zachary lately, but Terra had never seen her look happier. Next came Terra's turn. She wore an elegant, pink-trimmed, forest-green suit the Hoomes had made for her, and their magical jackets had found a new home in a leaf-patterned, button-up dress shirt. She didn't know if it still possessed the forest's magic in its weave, but she'd decided it wouldn't hurt to have a little magical help on her wedding day.

Her father walked her down the aisle. Cer had already done the same for Athene, at her daughter's insistence; she and Athene had wanted to remove some of the inherent sexism in fathers giving their daughters away, after all. Sadly, Terra's own mother couldn't help them out with accomplishing that.

Up at the altar, Terra took in Athene's effervescent, glowing beauty. She was dressed in a loose, rose-colored gown that skimmed her body and stopped at her ankles with a delicate lace hem, which the Hoomes had apparently spent hours perfecting. How they had gone about making their wedding clothes, Terra didn't know. The petite, gray-haired women had kept her and Athene out of the room allocated to them for their work, telling them that seeing their clothes before their wedding day was bad luck. Terra had never heard this custom before, but she just went with it. After all, she would soon be getting married, and the rest was just second fiddle to that wonderful fact.

After the witch and high priestess leading the ceremony had spoken, it was time for them to exchange vows, and Terra's voice shook a little as she read hers. It wasn't shaking from fear, but from her joyful tears that came as she poured out her heart to her soon-to-be wife.

"I had always wondered," she began, "if there was some spell you could cast to bring you someone who would love you, someone who would love you above all else. I would have searched throughout the land to find something that I thought of as so useful, as so very important. But then, this beautiful woman standing before me caught my eye one night, and I realized only weeks later that I didn't need a magic word to bring me that love. Because now I had one—the word was 'Athene.'"

Terra continued from there, but everything else she had to say was less important than those beginning words. The rest of her speech seemed almost unnecessary now, but once she had finished, she looked up, and Athene was crying, too.

"And you are *my* magic word, Terra," Athene said through her tears. She pulled Terra close, holding her in her arms in a hug that wasn't really a planned part of the ceremony. But magic can rarely be planned either, Terra thought, nor can love. And magic and love, she thought, as she held her lover ever-so-close, would always be a perfect pair...just like her and Athene.

About the Author

Maggie Morton lives in Northern California with her partner and their two cats. She is the winner of an Alice B. Award 2013 Lavender Certificate for her first novel, the lesbian, erotic romance *Dreaming of Her*. This is her second novel.

Books Available from Bold Strokes Books

Love and Devotion by Jove Belle. KC Hall trips her way through life, stumbling into an affair with a married bombshell twice her age. Thankfully, her best friend, Emma Reynolds, is there to show her the true meaning of Love and Devotion. (978-1-60282-965-7)

Rush by Carsen Taite. Murder, secrets, and romance combine to create the ultimate rush. (978-1-60282-966-4)

The Shoal of Time by J.M. Redmann. It sounded too easy. Micky Knight is reluctant to take the case because the easy ones often turn into the hard ones, and the hard ones turn into the dangerous ones. In this one, easy turns hard without warning. (978-1-60282-967-1)

In Between by Jane Hoppen. At the age of 14, Sophie Schmidt discovers that she was born an intersexual baby and sets off on a journey to find her place in a world that denies her true existence. (978-1-60282-968-8)

Secret Lies by Amy Dunne. While fleeing from her abuser, Nicola Jackson bumps into Jenny O'Connor, and their unlikely friendship quickly develops into a blossoming romance—but when it comes down to a matter of life or death, are they both willing to face their fears? (978-1-60282-970-1)

Under Her Spell by Maggie Morton. The magic of love brought Terra and Athene together, but now a magical quest stands between them—a quest for Athene's hand in marriage. Will their passion keep them together, or will stronger magic tear them apart? (978-1-60282-973-2)

Homestead by Radclyffe. R. Clayton Sutter figures getting NorthAm Fuel's newest refinery operational on a rolling tract of land in Upstate New York should take a month or two, but then, she hadn't counted on local resistance in the form of vandalism, petitions, and one furious farmer named Tess Rogers. (978-1-60282-956-5)

Battle of Forces: Sera Toujours by Ali Vali. Kendal and Piper return to New Orleans to start the rest of eternity together, but the return of an old enemy makes their peaceful reunion short-lived, especially when they join forces with the new queen of the vampires. (978-1-60282-957-2)

How Sweet It Is by Melissa Brayden. Some things are better than chocolate. Molly O'Brien enjoys her quiet life running the bakeshop in a small town. When the beautiful Jordan Tuscana returns home, Molly can't deny the attraction—or the stirrings of something more. (978-1-60282-958-9)

The Missing Juliet: A Fisher Key Adventure by Sam Cameron. A teenage detective and her friends search for a kidnapped Hollywood star in the Florida Keys. (978-1-60282-959-6)

Amor and More: Love Everafter edited by Radclyffe and Stacia Seaman. Rediscover favorite couples as Bold Strokes Books authors reveal glimpses of life and love beyond the honeymoon in short stories featuring main characters from favorite BSB novels. (978-1-60282-963-3)

First Love by CJ Harte. Finding true love is hard enough, but for Jordan Thompson, daughter of a conservative president, it's challenging, especially when that love is a female rodeo cowgirl. (978-1-60282-949-7)

Pale Wings Protecting by Lesley Davis. Posing as a couple to investigate the abduction of infants, Special Agent Blythe Kent and Detective Daryl Chandler find themselves drawn into a battle over the innocents, with demons on one side and the unlikeliest of protectors on the other. (978-1-60282-964-0)

Mounting Danger by Karis Walsh. Sergeant Rachel Bryce, an outcast on the police force, is put in charge of the department's newly formed mounted division. Can she and polo champion Callan Lanford resist their growing attraction as they struggle to safeguard the disaster-prone unit? (978-1-60282-951-0)

Meeting Chance by Jennifer Lavoie. When man's best friend turns on Aaron Cassidy, the teen keeps his distance until fate puts Chance in his hands. (978-1-60282-952-7)

At Her Feet by Rebekah Weatherspoon. Digital marketing producer Suzanne Kim knows she has found the perfect love in her new mistress Pilar, but before they can make the ultimate commitment, Suzanne's professional life threatens to disrupt their perfectly balanced bliss. (978-1-60282-948-0)

Show of Force by AJ Quinn. A chance meeting between navy pilot Evan Kane and correspondent Tate McKenna takes them on a roller-coaster ride where the stakes are high, but the reward is higher: a chance at love. (978-1-60282-942-8)

Clean Slate by Andrea Bramhall. Can Erin and Morgan work through their individual demons to rediscover their love for each other, or are the unexplainable wounds too deep to heal? (978-1-60282-943-5)

Hold Me Forever by D. Jackson Leigh. An investigation into illegal cloning in the quarter horse racing industry threatens to destroy the growing attraction between Georgia debutante Mae St. John and Louisiana horse trainer Whit Casey. (978-1-60282-944-2)

Trusting Tomorrow by PJ Trebelhorn. Funeral director Logan Swift thinks she's perfectly happy with her solitary life devoted to helping others cope with loss until Brooke Collier moves in next door to care for her elderly grandparents. (978-1-60282-891-9)

Forsaking All Others by Kathleen Knowles. What if what you think you want is the opposite of what makes you happy? (978-1-60282-892-6)

Exit Wounds by VK Powell. When Officer Loane Landry falls in love with ATF informant Abigail Mancuso, she realizes that nothing is as it seems—not the case, not her lover, not even the dead. (978-1-60282-893-3)

Dirty Power by Ashley Bartlett. Cooper's been through hell and back, and she's still broke and on the run. But at least she found the twins. They'll keep her alive. Right? (978-1-60282-896-4)

The Rarest Rose by I. Beacham. After a decade of living in her beloved house, Ele disturbs its past and finds her life being haunted by the presence of a ghost who will show her that true love never dies. (978-1-60282-884-1)

Code of Honor by Radclyffe. The face of terror is hard to recognize—especially when it's homegrown. The next book in the Honor series. (978-1-60282-885-8)

Does She Love You? by Rachel Spangler. When Annabelle and Davis find out they are both in a relationship with the same woman, it leaves them facing life-altering questions about trust, redemption, and the possibility of finding love in the wake of betrayal. (978-1-60282-886-5)

The Road to Her by KE Payne. Sparks fly when actress Holly Croft, star of UK soap Portobello Road, meets her new on-screen love interest, the enigmatic and sexy Elise Manford. (978-1-60282-887-2)

Shadows of Something Real by Sophia Kell Hagin. Trying to escape flashbacks and nightmares, ex-POW Jamie Gwynmorgan stumbles into the heart of former Red Cross worker Adele Sabellius and uncovers a deadly conspiracy against everything and everyone she loves. (978-1-60282-889-6)

Date with Destiny by Mason Dixon. When sophisticated bank executive Rashida Ivey meets unemployed blue collar worker Destiny Jackson, will her life ever be the same? (978-1-60282-878-0)

The Devil's Orchard by Ali Vali. Cain and Emma plan a wedding before the birth of their third child while Juan Luis is still lurking, and as Cain plans for his death, an unexpected visitor arrives and challenges her belief in her father, Dalton Casey. (978-1-60282-879-7)

Secrets and Shadows by L.T. Marie. A bodyguard and the woman she protects run from a madman and into each other's arms. (978-1-60282-880-3)

Change Horizons: Three Novellas by Gun Brooke. Three stories of courageous women who dare to love as they fight to claim a future in a hostile universe. (978-1-60282-881-0)

Scarlet Thirst by Crin Claxton. When hot, feisty Rani meets cool, vampire Rob, one lifetime isn't enough, and the road from human to vampire is shorter than you think... (978-1-60282-856-8)

Battle Axe by Carsen Taite. How close is too close? Bounty hunter Luca Bennett will soon find out. (978-1-60282-871-1)

Improvisation by Karis Walsh. High school geometry teacher Jan Carroll thinks she's figured out the shape of her life and her future, until graphic artist and fiddle player Tina Nelson comes along and teaches her to improvise. (978-1-60282-872-8)

For Want of a Fiend by Barbara Ann Wright. Without her Fiendish power, can Princess Katya and her consort Starbride stop a magic-wielding madman from sparking an uprising in the kingdom of Farraday? (978-1-60282-873-5)

Broken in Soft Places by Fiona Zedde. The instant Sara Chambers meets the seductive and sinful Merille Thompson, she falls hard, but knowing the difference between love and a dangerous, all-consuming desire is just one of the lessons Sara must learn before it's too late. (978-1-60282-876-6)

Healing Hearts by Donna K. Ford. Running from tragedy, the women of Willow Springs find that with friendship, there is hope, and with love, there is everything. (978-1-60282-877-3)